All Hung Up

A Bluegrass Single Novella

Kathleen Brooks

Prologue

Keeneston, Kentucky
Seven years ago . . .

"I am not a tart!" Taylor Jefferies stomped her foot in anger. Taylor used all the training that made her an Academy Award-winning actress to continue yelling at the sweet old people in front of her.

Taylor had just arrived in the quaint little town of Keeneston that week to visit Cy Davies, the man who was like an uncle to her, before starting her freshman year of college. It turned out the man who had taught a sixteen-year-old how to be an adult wasn't at all what he appeared to be.

When a ruthless black-market dealer kidnapped the woman Cy loved, the kind people of Keeneston had turned into warriors. Women old enough to be her grandmother, soccer moms, and professionals all gathered at the Blossom Café to develop a plan to help "one of their own."

So, here she was, dressed in daisy dukes, a bustier that pushed her ample breasts out, and a pair of stripper heels, screaming at the three old Rose sisters who owned the local bed and breakfast and the Blossom Café. They were the distraction so Cy could rescue Gemma, the woman he loved. And what a distraction they were. All the guards surrounding the mansion where Gemma was being held were standing on the driveway watching the scene the people of Keeneston were acting out.

Trey Everett, the cute boy that Uncle Cy had introduced to Taylor earlier that week, wrapped his large strong arms around her as gunfire filled the night air.

Trey held Taylor tight against him. He was ready to throw her behind him if anything happened. He had been so nervous just to be introduced to the blonde bombshell the other day that it had taken Trey stuttering his way through a tour of the town before he could formulate a full sentence. Somehow it made it worse that Taylor was just a year younger than his nineteen years. She'd done and seen so much in her life while the most Trey could say was that he was a running back at Vanderbilt University. Playing in the Southeast Conference didn't quite hold up to winning an Oscar.

"Look!" Taylor's bright red lips whispered as she grabbed his hand in hers.

Trey almost shook himself. He was holding America's Sweetheart, Taylor Jefferies, against his chest and she had just grabbed his hand. His body reacted instantly, but Trey just tried to take a mental snapshot of this moment. It wasn't like she was actually interested in a small-town country boy like him.

"Cy! Gemma!" Taylor raced from his hold and rushed to hug the couple emerging from the mansion. Trey was relieved they were safe, but he'd be lying if he didn't feel the loss of Taylor from his arms. He may only be a sophomore in college, but he knew something special when he saw it. And Taylor Jefferies was definitely something special.

Trey approached quietly as the town embraced Cy and Gemma. Taylor was still bouncing around as she told them of the diversion they had created. Cy's hazel eyes searched the crowd and locked onto Trey's. A smile graced his face before Cy gave a little nod of thanks to Trey. He knew what it was for. He'd kept Taylor safe during their little stunt. At least he'd always have that with her.

Trey turned to leave. Cy and Gemma were in the capable hands of the town.

"Where you going? Aren't you going to celebrate?" Trey knew that voice. He turned and caught sight of Taylor's blonde hair, big blue eyes, huge . . . assets, and those short shorts. Her legs seemed to go on for miles. She wasn't just out of his league; he wasn't even in the same sport!

"I was going to head home to start packing for Vandy. I have to be down there in a couple days for football camp."

"Mind if I come with you?"

Trey felt his brow crease in confusion. "You want to come with *me?*"

Taylor laughed and Trey had never seen anything more beautiful. "Yes. I'm too excited to go back to Miss Lily's bed and breakfast. I thought we could finish up our tour. You mentioned something about a fishing pond."

Trey felt his head nod and Taylor flashed him a smile before linking her fingers with his. He shook his head, trying to clear it. He must have been hit on the head. Yes, that was it. He'd received a blow to the head and he was in a coma at the hospital. This was all just a dream.

It's just a dream, Trey repeated to himself as he helped Taylor down from his old pick-up truck. He watched in wonder as she looked around the small clearing and took in his favorite fishing pond.

"This place is amazing. I'm so jealous you got to grow up here."

"Jealous? Of me? You're America's Sweetheart," Trey babbled. Smooth, Everett, real smooth.

Taylor slipped off the heels she was wearing and climbed on a large rock on the bank of the pond. She dangled a toe over the water and the happy-go-lucky attitude seemed to slip down her body and into the water.

"You know how much I would have killed for a life like yours?" she asked so quietly that Trey had to climb up next to her in order to hear. Of course he had to stop thinking of her legs in those shorts and her breasts . . . Listen, Everett!

"Why would you want that? You got to travel the world, be on the cover of magazines, and star in movies. It's amazing what you've accomplished."

"True. I've done more than most actors have ever dreamed of. I have more money that I could ever spend in my lifetime and access to anything I could ever want. But the one thing I wanted I'll never have."

Trey couldn't help but pull her against him as a single tear fell into the water below. Suddenly he felt very protective of the girl he could only dream of having in his life.

"I wanted my family. But they were too concerned about getting their hands on my money to care about me as a person. They pushed and pushed until I hated what I was doing. I had to sue my own parents. That's not something I'm proud of. Luckily, Cy was there to help me. He was there to show me how to save the money I was earning. He was there to teach me how to cook and how to drive the used SUV he convinced me to buy. He gave me the closest thing to a normal life I could have. I know I could have gone out and bought a sports car or mansion and hit the clubs every night, but Cy sat me down and explained to me about wasting my time, talent, and money on things like that."

"It sounds like you did have a family. And the Davies family is the best family you could have," Trey said quietly as he brushed back her hair from her face.

"And now he's got Gemma. I'm not jealous," Taylor said quickly. "I'm really happy for them, but I'm part of his old life. He has a future here and I'm not sure I fit in." Trey felt her silently cry against his shoulder as he held her. His heart hurt for her and he felt so helpless. He couldn't solve this problem for her. All he could do was hold her as she cried.

"Shh, it's okay, Taylor. Cy won't forget about you. You're very much part of his past, present, and future."

"It's not just that. I'm scared, Trey."

"But you have nothing to be scared of, Taylor. Cy won't forget about you. I'm sure of it."

"College. I'm scared of going to college without Cy. Vanderbilt is a great school, but I've never been to school before. I don't know how to meet new people. Cy always introduced me around and made me feel included. I've never been to high school. I've never been in a class with other kids. I've never raised my hand to ask a question. I've never stepped foot in a school, period."

"Well, I'll be there. But I have a feeling you won't even remember me with all the friends you'll make. You may not know it, but you attract people with your smile. You're so genuine that people won't be able to help themselves. You'll have more friends than you know what to do with — as it should be."

Taylor rested her head against his shoulder and tossed

a stone into the pond. Trey watched the ripples flow outward and knew it could be the last time it would be like this with her. She'd hit campus like a whirlwind. People would be clamoring to be her friend and she certainly wouldn't have time for a nobody like him.

Country music filled the air as cups were lifted to salute the band. Taylor felt the cell phones snapping pictures of her, but at least her fellow classmates were less intrusive than Hollywood's paparazzi. The longer she hung around campus and Nashville, the more people seemed to stop caring about her. In fact, she hardly noticed them anymore. And similarly, they noticed her less and less.

It was winter in Nashville but that didn't stop the miniskirts and cowboy boots from making an appearance tonight. Her first-ever set of final exams was done and now her sorority was celebrating. She'd joined as a way to put herself out there and meet people. It had worked and she had made some real friends and some not-so-real friends. But, at least she was experiencing life.

Taylor took a sip of her drink and looked around the packed place. It was then she saw him — Trey Everett. She hadn't been this close to him since that night by the pond. After he drove her back to the bed and breakfast, he'd given her a first real kiss. It was quick, just a gentle touch of his lips to hers. But it had been the first that wasn't on a movie set with directors telling her what to do.

As she sat in her room that night, she'd talked herself out of the special night that had happened. She picked up the paper the next day expecting to find her sob story in black and white–except it wasn't there. She had scoured the online gossip sites for a month, but nothing ever appeared. By the time school started, she was halfway to thinking Trey hung the moon. He had her trust and a good chunk of her heart.

She'd worn jeans, a Vandy sweatshirt, and baseball cap low over her face for his football games. He'd been spectacular. She cheered every play he ran and cringed with every hit he took. She thought about calling him, but what would she say? "Hi, Trey. I've been thinking of you every day since that night by the pond. Have you been thinking of me, too?" And then there was football. He was in the zone. Sports reporters were starting to talk about him. And national awards were being mentioned when they said his name.

Taylor glanced across the room and her suspicions were confirmed. He had women crawling on him. And who could blame them. Heck, she wanted to climb on him, too. He was six-foot-two-inches tall, two hundred and twenty pounds of muscle, and a smile sweet enough to melt you on the spot. He was a gentleman through and through. The college paper constantly remarked about him holding doors for women and spending time at the hospital with patients. Sure, she did the same, but they never seemed to be there at the same time. It seemed fate had said no to her wish that he'd notice her again.

Setting her drink on the bar, she turned to watch one of her sorority sisters hitting on the bartender. It was under twenty-one night and he was having none of it. But it was amusing to watch nonetheless.

Someone moved to the seat next to her so she moved to give him room without even looking as she continued to watch the show. "Sometimes, when you don't even try, is when you're the most beautiful."

Taylor's breath caught as she turned in her chair and came face to face with Trey Everett. "Trey!"

She saw him chuckle and wanted to throw herself in his arms. "I'm surprised you remember my name. All the guys were talking about you. They didn't believe me when I told them I met you this summer. Thanks for not making me look like a loser in front of the team."

"Of course I remember you. You're the one person here I know I can trust. I've actually thought about you quite a lot, but didn't want to bother you during football season. You have a lot going on."

"You'd never bother me, Taylor. How have you been?"

Taylor's heart flipped in her chest. "I've been good. I've gone to all of your football games."

Taylor saw the surprised look on Trey's face and then a huge smile spread across her face. She found herself looking at his lips again and remembering the kiss. She'd been kissed since that night, but no one could ever live up to Trey's simple caress.

"You've been to my games? Why didn't you tell me? I would have gotten you tickets."

"I think I can afford my own tickets. Besides, you need to focus if you want to win the Heisman."

"I know you can afford your own tickets, Taylor. But, I would like to have done it for you anyway. Thank you for coming; that means a lot to me." Trey's hand covered hers and gave it a little squeeze.

"Well, sign me up for the bowl then. I would love to go. Are you all here to celebrate your bowl invitation?"

"I will." Trey's face lit up before turning sheepish. "And yeah. The guys were talking about you. I might have mentioned that you were a really nice person and then they bet me I didn't know you. I know you have your sorority and I'm sure a boyfriend, but it was also a good excuse to see you again."

"Well, you're right and wrong. It is good to see you again, but I don't have a boyfriend. The guys around here haven't lived up to my expectations."

"Oh," Trey's face fell as he gave her a weak smile. "Well, I better get back to the team."

"Do you know why they don't live up?" Taylor asked quickly as she put her hand on his, stopping him from getting up.

"Why?"

"Because no one has taken me to a pond as a date." Taylor almost laughed as Trey registered what she was saying.

"So, you're telling me . . ."

"I'm telling you to kiss me, Trey."

"Yes, ma'am," Trey grinned. He pulled off his Vandy baseball hat and ran his fingers through his dark blond hair before bending forward and slowly putting his lips to hers. Taylor felt the warmth spread from her lips to her heart. His team whistled and cheered, but she didn't hear it. She didn't care about the cameras flashing or the headlines in tomorrow's papers. She just cared that Trey was pulling her against his hard body and deepening the kiss.

Chapter One

Trey Everett ran his hand over his aching thigh muscle and stared out at the ocean. He'd been in the NFL for four years now, but summer was always the worst. In the summer you had to get back into shape before the season opened. Suddenly all those burgers you ate and those exercises you decided to skip didn't seem worth the pain he was going through now. The screen door to the beach house slammed shut and the sound of Taylor's bare feet walking through the sand reached him.

"Here, have some coffee. It'll get you going for practice," Taylor smiled as she handed him a large to-go cup of coffee.

After being together six and a half years, she knew his routine. He couldn't have asked for a better woman to stand by him every day. But Trey still had to pinch himself when he looked at her. There was no question about it—he didn't believe he deserved her. Having just turned twenty-five, she was even more stunning than when he met her in Keeneston seven years ago. She'd matured in all the right ways physically. Her hips curved in a way that begged his hand to cup them. Her long blonde hair flowed down her back. It was so erotic spread out on the pillow every night. But it was how she'd matured mentally that he loved the most.

While Trey had been an All-American his senior year and been drafted into the NFL, Taylor had opted to stay at Vandy to get her degree in film. She studied hard and took summer classes in order to graduate early. While she finished school, Trey had been a fairly high draft pick and headed to the newly formed Georgia Vultures. At least the sweet but clueless owners had been talked into naming the team the Vultures over the Fighting Peaches, but they were still the worst team in the NFL. Not to mention the butt of every mascot joke possible.

As soon as Taylor graduated, she moved into a small apartment near the football stadium and enrolled in the local university for a Masters program in Business. Every day after practice, Trey came home and was surprised to see Taylor was still there. He didn't know what she saw in him. When her books started taking up most of the apartment and when she started talking about forming a company, Trey knew they had to move. Both had jumped at the chance to buy the beach house on Hung Island, just across the bridge from the stadium. Sure, it was a quirky place to live, but they had all the privacy they wanted and nothing was more relaxing than sitting on their swing after a long day and pretending the ocean was their own little pond.

"Are you excited about filming at Seawave Resort today?" Trey asked as he wrapped an arm around her waist, drawing her to his side.

"More like petrified. I can't believe you let me start my own film company. What do I know about producing? Filming on location for Grant's scenes were a nightmare and now we're adding Melanie to the mix. Her agent has already called three times to complain about this and that," Taylor sighed.

"But you love it," Trey chuckled before taking a sip of coffee.

"But I love it. It's everything I've always wanted. Being behind the camera is surreal. I can really see the movie for the puzzle that it is. And it's such a good script. I shouldn't let Melanie bother me." Taylor paused and shook her head. "Did I tell you about the time I was fifteen and she 'accidently' stepped on my long skirt, causing it to fall off and me to flash the press corps?"

"Why did you hire her then?" Trey asked with concern filling his voice. He didn't like to think of anyone hurting Taylor. He knew how much she had gone through at the hands of her parents and the stresses that show business had taken on someone so young.

"I know how much of a diva she is, but she was perfect for this role. I'm a big girl now. I can take care of one self-centered actress in my sleep with both hands tied behind my back. Besides, I'm behind the camera, not in front of it now. Melanie loves being the star and I'm happy to step aside and let her do just that." Taylor looked down at her cell phone and sighed. "And it's time for you to get to practice and gossip with all the guys," she teased.

Trey looked offended as he put his hand to his heart. "Men do not gossip. We do manly things like lift lots of weights and grunt."

Taylor rolled her eyes. "You men gossip more than the Rose sisters at the Blossom Café."

"With that insult, I'm going to practice." Trey gave her a playful tug, turning her to be enclosed in his arms. He loved the feel of her body against his. Lowering his lips, he took his time kissing her goodbye.

Trey pulled onto Hangman's Highway and drove along the loop that went around the island until he came to Treasure Trail. Glancing at his mirrors, he made sure he wasn't being followed as he headed toward downtown. The small shop came up on his right before he hit Main Street, the only other road on Hung Island. Looking around before he got out of his truck, he made sure no one saw him as he hurried into the shop.

"Hello, Trey. We got what you want right here," the woman in flip-flops and jean shorts said as she reached under the counter.

"Thanks, June. How did it turn out?"

"See for yourself." June opened the small blue box and Trey nervously looked down at the large diamond he'd picked out for Taylor. It was perfect in its simplicity, just like her.

"It's perfect. Thank you, June."

Trey's hand shook as he picked up the small, delicate box and put it in his pocket. He kept his hand on it the whole time as he made his way to the car. He was petrified there would suddenly be a hole in his pocket and it would fall out. Or what if it traveled all the way out of his pocket and fell onto the street?

When he got in the car, he put the box in the cup holder and kept half an eye on it until he reached Captain's Bridge. As he crossed the only bridge off the island, he rolled up his windows and kept his hand over the box. Somehow he feared a wind gust would lift the box from the car and hurl it out the window and into the ocean. He knew he was being irrational, but that box and what was in it symbolized too much for him to take a chance at losing it.

Trey parked at the stadium and clutched it again in his pocket as he made his way to the locker room. When he pushed open the heavy door, he was met with the smell of manliness, or as Taylor called it, stinky sweat.

"Everett, afraid your dick will fall off?" Morris, the center on the offensive line, yelled as he slipped on a practice jersey.

Trey pulled his hand out of his pocket and the room fell quiet as the men moved forward to look at the pretty blue box in his hand. "I just picked this up today."

"What is it?" Morris asked as he pushed people out of the way. Trey opened the box and Morris stopped in his tracks.

"No way. You're not nearly good enough for someone like Taylor Jefferies."

"Bullcrap. My man here has more touchdown runs than anyone else in the league. I say she's not good enough for him . . . wait!" Tucker, the team quarterback, pulled out his phone and pulled up Taylor's *To the Max* magazine cover. She had just turned eighteen and was in barely-there lingerie. "I take that back. She's way too good for you!"

The team broke into laughter and Trey rolled his eyes as he carefully placed the ring inside his locker. "I know that. Why do you think it's taken me so long to propose? But someone like her deserves the perfect proposal."

"How are you doing to do it? Mine at halftime against Florida was pretty cool," Morris puffed up as he bragged.

"It was, but I want to do something that no one else has done. I have the perfect night planned. She's shooting her movie on the island, so she's away from home a lot right now. I'm going to cover the place in rose petals. After cooking her the perfect dinner, I'm going to propose."

"Not original, but that's smooth," Tucker said as he tied

his cleats.

"Not as smooth as Johnson's up in Boston. Remember that one? Had our wives and girlfriends complaining for months we weren't *romantic* enough," Christian, one of the wide receivers, complained.

"But what did it get him?" Morris asked rhetorically.

"Laid!" Christian joked.

"Wait, you haven't heard?" Morris said with obvious glee.

"Haven't heard what?" Trey asked as he pulled off his shirt.

"Johnson's getting a divorce."

"No!" The room gasped as Morris went into full detail of the scandal leading up to the divorce.

"That's nothing," Tucker said, quieting the room once again. "Did you hear the coach for the Prey has been sexting with . . ."

"Gentlemen!" Coach Krupp called out, silencing the locker room immediately. "What's this about sexting?"

Trey followed the group out onto the field and banished the image of them all with white tufts of hair like the Rose sisters. They weren't nearly that bad. Besides, they weren't gossiping; they were just staying current.

"I bet you a hundred bucks that Johnson . . ." Trey heard called out. Okay, so maybe they were a little like the Rose sisters, but he'd die before telling Taylor that she was right.

Chapter Two

Taylor slipped into her skinny jeans and flowing white blouse. She slid on her ballet flats and looked at herself in the mirror. She took in a deep breath and tried to push aside her fear of the past. The more she'd been in the spotlight, the more her parents had pushed. They'd demanded money, attention, and perks. It was never enough. They had wanted to be her to the point she felt like a prostitute for them. When she'd discovered millions of dollars missing and her parents high on cocaine in a house she'd bought and paid for, she'd had enough.

At sixteen, she'd turned to the stuntman who had always looked out for her for help. Cy Davies had helped her become emancipated from her parents. She had made the mistake of thinking that would be the end of her problems, but it wasn't. It was only the beginning. Managers, promoters, and directors—they all thought they could step in and control her. If it hadn't been for Cy's guidance in picking the right people to surround her, it would be scary to think where she'd be now.

When she'd turned seventeen, she won an Oscar, and it had changed her life. Professionally, she gained a lot of respect. But then her parents had found her as she left her studio alone right before her eighteenth birthday. Her father refused to move from in front of her car as her mother screamed, ranted, and pounded on the car windows.

"You'd be nothing without us! You're worthless! We made you and you cut us off as if we're nobodies. You ungrateful child!" Taylor could still hear the screaming echoing in her mind.

She had gotten out of the car to try to contain a scene that was quickly spiraling out of control. Tourists had taken out their cameras, and Taylor started to feel each snap of the camera and each whisper closing in on her, mocking her.

"Mom, please. You're high. I'll pay for rehab," Taylor had begged. Her mother responded with a hard slap across her face. Pain and heat blossomed across her cheek. Silent tears fell as her mother reached up to hit her again. Security came rushing into the street and pulled her mother away.

Cy's arms were around her as the world blurred. All she heard, all she saw, all she felt were the cameras as people pushed in on her. While security handcuffed her parents and quietly collected the cameras from the tourists who would be paid off, Cy kept the dizziness from overtaking her. Her parents were placed in a police car and Taylor pulled all her courage together to walk over to the cruiser. With her cheek bright red from the hit, she leaned down and looked at her parents. "I never want to see you again. You will never see another cent from me. If you ever touch me again, I'll press criminal charges. Goodbye forever."

The next day she'd shown up on the set of her new movie and sat in the makeup chair. She felt nothing. The excitement of being a movie star was gone. But when she stepped in front of the camera, all she saw were flashing bulbs and people closing in on her. Her head spun and the next thing she knew she was waking up in her dressing room. She knew right then she was done with Hollywood. Taylor left the studio and the town forever. Her hands shook and fear thundered through her as she hurried from the set.

Taylor pulled out of the movie with the excuse of attending college. For the first two years, she'd taken all her required courses and loved learning. But something had been missing. When her sorority needed a video made for Greek Week, she hesitantly agreed to direct it. It was the best thing she'd ever done. She knew without a doubt that being in control of filming was what she wanted. There was no fear when she was behind the camera. Thoughts of film companies swirled in her head. She wanted her own to run. She wanted to hire the perfect people for the parts, not the ones who kissed the most ass. Once she knew what she wanted, she went after it.

Everyone patted her on her head thinking she was just doing this as a little hobby. Everyone except Trey. Trey not only supported her, he moved them into a house with her own office and made her dinner every night for two months while she read scripts, books, and researched the industry news. It was then she found the book she wanted and started raising the money needed to get her first project started. It was also Trey who told her she could do it when she doubted herself. It was Trey who helped her raise the last funds needed to get the project started. She didn't know how she got so lucky to find a man who genuinely supported her. And he actually encouraged her to reach for the stars and beyond. And knowing that he would be there to catch her if she failed only gave her the courage to reach further.

Looking in the mirror, Taylor nodded to herself. She

was ready. Taylor grabbed her purse and script before heading out the door to start the first day of principal shooting.

Taylor pulled up to the Seawave Resort and Hotel on the far side of the island and looked around in shock. The resort itself was breathtaking with precision landscaping and a mansion that had been converted into a hotel. The crashing waves of the Atlantic Ocean served as a perfect backdrop. Taylor always thought it reminded her of what *The Great Gatsby*'s set would be like if set in the South. But today it wasn't the resort that had her attention. It was the people around the old mansion. She hadn't counted on media being there. Cameras were flashing and a small group of fans had gathered for autographs. Melanie was already in full make-up, taking pictures and talking to reporters. Figures. Melanie would run naked around the hotel if she thought it would get her press.

Surprisingly, Grant was nowhere to be found. Taylor scanned the grounds looking for her lead actor. The cameras were in position off to the side of the hotel. The outdoor café was set up, and the extras were milling around in their 1960s attire. Taking a deep breath, Taylor slid the strap of her bag over her shoulder and stepped out of her car. Instantly, reporters started to call her name and wave her over. Taylor smiled and headed their way as she tried to control her breathing. It wasn't rational, but it was still hard for her to be in front of cameras again.

"Miss Jefferies! Miss Jefferies!" Taylor let out a breath and relaxed a little as she approached Millie Michaels, the reporter for the Hung Island's *Treasure Trove* newspaper.

"Hi, Millie. Miss Jefferies? Really?" Taylor asked the woman fresh out of journalism school. Her brown hair was tied back in a ponytail and she stood with her smartphone held out like the other reporters. Only the other reporters weren't wearing a shirt that read *Hung like a Pirate* over jean shorts.

"Well, I thought I should be all professional and stuff," Millie replied with a shrug.

Taylor smiled and congratulated herself on not laughing out loud. "Nice shirt."

"I thought you'd appreciate it, since I won it off you at poker last month. Next I'm raising the stakes to get your Oscar."

"I don't think that will be on the table, even if I run out of cash again. But I'll give you first dibs at questioning me about the movie right now as long as you don't print the picture of me twerking after losing that last hand."

"Deal," Millie grinned. Then the smile was replaced with a serious look and the phone was held out again. "I'm Millie Michaels with *Treasure Trove* newspaper. I'm here with Academy Award-winning actress-turned-producer Taylor Jefferies. Taylor, how does it feel to be back in the movie business after a seven-year break?"

"It feels great. I'm loving being behind the camera and am honored that the famous Jim Peters is taking the time to guide me in directing."

"Mr. Peters is known for his crazy antics on set along with his four Best Director statues. He is rumored to have once put a snake in the purse of an actress to get a believable shot of fear and surprise from her. Has he done anything like that on any of your sets before?"

"Jim is known for his antics, but I've never seen him resort to any such extreme measures. And I doubt we'll have to. We have a fabulous cast." Taylor tried not to choke on her words while Melanie stared daggers at her.

Reporters had moved away from Melanie and were all holding out their recorders in Taylor's direction.

"Can you tell us a little about the movie and the actors in the starring roles?" Millie asked as she elbowed a reporter from one of those entertainment shows out of the way.

"Sure. The film is a love story set during the Vietnam War. Grant Elliott is playing Darin, a reporter covering the effects of the war on the young men being drafted and the women they were leaving behind. Kathy is a young woman bucking the tradition of getting married straight out of high school. She's moved away from home and to the big city where she went to college. Melanie Grace is perfect for the part and is going to really bring Kathy's character to life.

"The movie follows these two as they meet at a restaurant when Kathy's a student, and love blossoms during this run-in even though they don't know each other's names. The two meet again briefly as Kathy is on her way to a new job at this resort. She leaves only knowing his first name. The film continues as Darin searches for Kathy."

Millie nodded her head and threw another elbow at the plastic-looking reporter from the entertainment show. "It sounds different from the dramas you used to star in. Why did you decide to go with a romance for your first movie?"

"When I read Gemma Davies's book, it spoke to me. I could see it and I couldn't get the story out of my head. One day, after Kathy and her best friend swear off men after a particularly bad date, there is a knock at the door and a dozen red roses from Darin appear. He never even knew her last name, but he'd found her all the way across the state. There's drama, there's laughter, and there's a happily ever after. What more could you want?" Taylor asked rhetorically.

"Speaking of happily ever after, how is your relationship with NFL running back Trey Everett? Are there wedding bells in your future?" Millie asked before a microphone hit her in the head. Plastic reporter was getting her revenge.

Taylor stepped back as she felt panic rising. It was the pushing, the shoving, and all the lights from the cameras that were upsetting her. She needed to end this interview quickly. "Trey and I are wonderful. Thank you for asking. Go Vultures! Get your season tickets now. I know I'll be there cheering them on. Thanks, Millie. See you all later!"

Taylor waved and plastered a shaky smile on her face before walking towards the set. She took the last sip of her coffee, threw the cup in the dumpster, and took a deep breath. She'd survived the cameras, but she was starting to shake. An orange blur leapt from behind the reporters and over the security fence, causing Taylor to jump away and let out a shriek. The streak of orange disappeared into the dumpster while security rushed forward. The woman with orange hair and a bright yellow shirt reappeared triumphantly with Taylor's coffee cup in her hand.

"Miss Jefferies, Miss Jefferies, can you sign this?" the woman with pigtails called out as security hauled her out the dumpster.

Taylor's heart resumed its normal beating and she shook her head. It had been a long time since she'd been around fans.

"What the hell?" Melanie asked as she stopped next to Taylor and stared at the woman being held in place by two guards.

"A fan," Taylor shrugged. It was better than the men who had tried to sneak into her trailer and steal her underwear.

"Why don't I have a fan doing that?" Melanie asked her assistant as the media focused on the woman in yellow calling out to Taylor.

"I'm your number one fan!" the crazed woman yelled.

"I'll see you on set. If someone's willing to jump in the dumpster and risk going to jail, then the least I can do is sign the stupid cup." Taylor set a soft smile on her face and indicated to the guards to bring the yellow dot of a woman to the fence.

"Oh my gosh, I can't believe I'm this close to you. I love you. I'm seriously your biggest fan. I just knew you'd be back." The woman who Taylor guessed to be around twenty-three gushed as Taylor dug around her bag for a pen.

"Well, it's nice to be back."

"I'm Cynthia Luisa Olson, but you can make it out to Cyndi Lu." the woman practically bounced as the guards held onto her shoulders.

"Here you go. Thanks, Cyndi Lu. Have a good day." Taylor handed the cup back to the woman as the guards hauled her away.

"Taylor!" A deep voice called from the far end of parking lot.

Taylor looked over her shoulder and her eyes went wide. Grant Elliott was running along the fence wearing nothing but athletic shorts. His toned and chiseled body shimmered in the morning sunlight as he rushed toward her with a worried look on his face. As he neared Taylor, she narrowed her eyes. Wait, his body wasn't shining with sweat. It was body oil. And was that make-up shadowing the contours of his abs to make them more defined? As Grant wrapped her up in a hug, she had her answer. Yup. It was make-up and this was all a big show for the reporters.

"Are you okay? I was so worried when I saw that mad woman leap at you."

"Grant, put me down or I'll kick you in the balls." Taylor could already read the headlines . . . *Is there romance on the set of Taylor Jefferies's new movie?*

"I was just worried, that's all."

"Damn." Taylor looked down at her shirt. "These oil stains better come out. And you know you weren't worried. You're just a camera whore. Can't you go after Melanie? She's single at least."

Grant didn't even look guilty as he shrugged and slung his arm over her shoulder. "Nope. She's not nearly as famous as you. Not half as pretty either. Come on, boss, let's get to work!" Grant slapped her bottom and raced into the make-up trailer before she could catch him. Yup, that was definitely going to be in the news. Taylor sighed. Welcome back to show biz.

Chapter Three

The smell coming from the oven made his mouth water. It was cooking perfectly. And thank goodness, because Taylor deserved nothing less than perfection. A look of relief came over Trey's face as he peeked into the oven. As soon as practice had ended, he had raced to the grocery and bought everything he needed for Taylor's favorite meal. The turtle brownies were baking, her favorite ice cream was in the freezer, the lobster just went in, the asparagus was ready, and the risotto was almost done.

Trey set the vase of flowers on the table and lit candles in the dining room. He grabbed a second bunch of roses and plucked the petals to spread on the ground in the shape of a big heart. Nervously, he went down on one knee as he heard the sound of a car parking outside. He pulled the ring out and waited for the love of his life to walk through the door. *Please say yes*, his mind chanted over and over as the door began to open.

"Taylor Jefferies . . . who the hell are you?" Trey asked the middle-aged couple walking through his door.

Trey tucked the engagement ring in his pocket and shot to his feet before approaching the angry-looking couple. Why would they be angry? It's his house they just walked into without knocking!

"Where is she?" The man with slightly graying, light

brown hair asked accusingly.

"Taylor!" The blonde woman in very tight clothes shrieked as she tried to run further into the house. Trey put out his arm and stopped her. Instead of stopping, she turned and started hitting him. "Assault! He's assaulting me. Call the police!"

"That's a fabulous idea. Then maybe I can figure out who you are and why you're breaking into my house."

"Mom? Dad?" Taylor's cold voice filled with disbelief sliced through the tantrum the lady was throwing.

"There you are, baby!" The woman pulled herself from Trey's grasp and ran for Taylor.

Trey's whole body went rigid as Taylor's eyes filled with anger and fear. Her mother wrapped her arms around Taylor and started sobbing. "My baby, my baby," she sobbed over and over as she clutched Taylor. Taylor, on the other hand, had a blank expression as she stood frozen in place while her mother bawled. Trey hurried over to her and pried her mother off her. The man she identified as her father slowly looked around the room as if he were casing the place for a robbery. He hadn't said anything to Taylor or Trey. Instead he stopped in front of Taylor's Oscar and stared.

"Get off me, you brute!" her mother screamed as she flailed in Trey's arms.

"Taylor?" He didn't know what to do. He knew what her parents had done to her, but she was just standing there. What was he supposed to do?

"Look here, honey. It's the Oscar we won for our ungrateful daughter," Taylor's father said as calmly as if he were pointing out a tourist attraction.

Taylor's mouth went dry at the sight of her parents. She

hadn't seen them since that horrible day at the studio when she was seventeen years old. They looked like her parents, but a little more wrinkled and worn down. She didn't really know what to do or think. Her mind literally froze with fear when her mother raced to her and gripped her in a tight hug.

But when her father held her Oscar and called her ungrateful, she finally managed to flinch. No matter what—the yelling, the degrading, or the verbal and physical abuse—Taylor still felt like a bad daughter when her father said these things. She knew in her mind she wasn't, but that didn't stop the guilt.

"That's it!" Trey roared, silencing the room.

Taylor watched as her mother stomped toward him and let her hand fly. Trey caught her wrist before her hand connected with his face and Taylor saw his square jaw tighten in anger. Flashbacks from her past threatened to overcome her, but it was Trey's powerful voice that brought her back to the present.

"You may do that to a defenseless child, but I'm neither a child nor defenseless. And neither is Taylor anymore. You're not welcome here. If you're not out of this house in five seconds, then I'm calling the police."

Taylor blinked and the room came back into focus. Trey was right. She wasn't alone anymore. She wasn't a child anymore. And she certainly wasn't defenseless anymore. "Why are you here? I told you I never wanted to see you again." Her voice was soft, but it held a tone of authority she was proud of.

"We're here for you, baby. To help you relaunch your career. We're your managers after all, baby," her mother cooed.

Her father put down the Oscar and wrapped his arm

around his wife. "That's right. And we're here to save you from this dumb jock. Running backs only have an average of three years in the NFL. His time is up. He'll be living off your money for the rest of his life. He's only holding you back. We saw you with Grant Elliott today. Now he's going places with his life. You would be a Hollywood power couple just like Brad and Angelina. You could be Graylor."

Her eyes shot to Trey. She hadn't told him yet about the show Grant put on this morning, but the quirk of his lips relaxed her. They'd always had trust in their relationship and she knew better than to think he'd fall for her parents' tricks.

"Graylor," Trey repeated. "They're right, Taylor. It sounds so much better than T2, T-Squared, Double T's and the other nicknames we have."

Taylor rolled her eyes and felt her confidence rise. She was not the person she was all those years ago. And one thing she knew for sure, there was no one she'd rather spend the rest of her life with, money or not, than Trey Everett. He made her stronger just with that little quirk of his lips.

"That's true. You were my managers. Ten percent, right?" Taylor asked as if she was trying to remember.

"That's right, baby," her mother smiled sweetly.

"Of course, now lots of managers make fifteen percent. But if you end up with Grant, and he makes us his manager, then we'll say what?" Her father shrugged. "Twelve percent each."

Taylor nodded her head. "Sorry, Trey, but we're done."

"I was worried about that. I mean, who can beat twelve percent? And Grant has those great abs."

Taylor couldn't stop herself; she laughed so hard tears fell as her parents stared at them confused. "Mom, Dad," she said as she laughed. "Get the hell out of our house. Oh, Trey, that was a good one. Do you know Grant has a make-up artist specifically for his abs?"

"I can't say I'm surprised. I can't wait to tell the guys. Their girlfriends and wives are always swooning over him," Trey said as he completely ignored her parents.

"See? I told you! Y'all are worse than the Rose sisters," Taylor laughed again.

"Nope. Not true," he denied before looking over at her parents and straightening to his full six-foot-two height. "I believe your daughter told you to get out." When they didn't move, he narrowed his eyes. "Now!" Upon hearing him yell, her parents narrowed their eyes in challenge. They never did like being told what to do.

"You don't give us orders!" her father yelled back.

"That's right," Taylor said as she walked past her parents and to the front door. "I do. And I'm telling you to leave and to never come back."

She held the front door open and waited silently until her parents walked out. Her mother turned and with the sweet smile Taylor used to fall for said, "We'll be around if you change your mind, baby. Mama loves you."

Taylor slammed the door as her answer and leaned against it completely worn out from the exchange. For a second, she closed her eyes and just breathed deeply. Her nose twitched. "Do I smell smoke?"

"Dang!" Trey rushed back into the kitchen and looked at the risotto burned to the pan, the overdone lobster, and the hard-as-a-rock brownies.

"You did this all for me?" Taylor asked in awe as Trey threw the whole pan into the trash.

"Yeah. I, um, wanted to celebrate your first day of filming. Why don't you go change . . . Is that oil on your shirt?"

"Grant." Taylor grinned. "I can't wait to tell you the story. The guys will love it."

"My lips are sealed. The guys will never know, but it sounds good. I'll clean this up and we can get some comfort food at the diner."

"I like that plan." Taylor rose on her tiptoes and kissed him. She dug her fingers into his strong shoulders and let the badness of the day fall away. "Oh, someone's happy I'm home," she chuckled as she rubbed herself against him.

"I sure am. But let's hurry before the tourists get there and take all the tables."

"You know Casey orders the locals to be served first. All it took was us living here full time for two years for her to grudgingly declare us not tourists."

"True, but I need to get this cleaned up. To be continued?"

"Definitely. I'll be right back. I just want to pretreat these oil stains."

Taylor sauntered from the room and Trey let out a worried breath. He reached into his pocket and pulled out the engagement ring box he had planned on giving her. As he threw the lobster out, he tossed away his idea for the perfect proposal happening tonight. Not with dinner blown and the confrontation with her parents—even if they had been right about one thing. He wasn't good enough for her. Giving one last disappointed look at the box, he reached up and set it behind the molding on top of the cabinet. It would be safe there until he could think of another perfect proposal.

Chapter Four

A block from the beach was Casey's Honkytonk Café. It was a dive and that was a compliment. But it also had the best food on the island. That made it worth putting up with the tourists in town for the stupid treasure hunt and Casey's not-so-sparkling personality. The crowd was large tonight and Taylor smiled at some of the production crew from the movie set as she made her way into the small diner.

"Local or tourist," a small blonde asked as she ran from table to table filling drinks.

"Nontourist," Casey shouted from behind the old-fashioned soda fountain.

"What do I do with that?" the little spitfire shot back to Casey.

"It means they're ahead of the tourists, but behind the locals," Casey fired back.

"I feel so loved, like part of the community. Thanks, Casey!" Trey called out before receiving the middle finger.

"This way." The new waitress grabbed two menus and the long line of tourists groaned as Trey and Taylor took the only empty table.

"New to Hung Island?" Taylor asked pleasantly. The blonde's head shot up and Taylor was met with huge blue eyes and a slightly shell-shocked look.

"Yup. I'm Reece. This is my first day . . . well, kinda, and I'll be taking care of you tonight. Give a shout when you know what you want."

"Will do. Welcome to the island, Reece," Taylor smiled. The poor girl. Starting a new job was never easy, but being a waitress during the peak of tourist season was brutal.

"So, tell me the story about Grant," Trey chuckled with anticipation.

She had been wrong; he was way worse than the Rose sisters when it came to gossip. Taylor launched into the story of Grant rushing to *save* her from the harmless, but slightly psychotic fan as a ploy to get on TV. "I swear, one of these days I am going to come to work and have to break up a scuffle between Grant and Melanie as they fight for camera time. They are attention whores in the worst way. But just be warned that some of the sketchier gossip sites have already picked up the story that we've broken up and I'm with Grant now."

Trey raised his hand and waved at Reece to let her know they were ready. "What is this, the sixth or seventh time we've broken up?" Trey asked as he grinned.

It had really bothered them when the first report came out. She had been in college and Trey had been training before his rookie season. But after discussing it, they were prepared when it happened again and again and again. "Seventh, I think."

Reece stopped at the table and gave them a quick smile. "Y'all ready?"

Trey nodded and Taylor placed her order for the fried pork chop while Trey ordered the shrimp and grits. Reece was writing down the order when talk of the treasure started up again from one of her cameramen a couple of tables away. "I'll get this out to you shortly," Reece said as she topped off their iced tea and headed to the next table.

Her cameraman saw her, smiled, and waved. "Hey, boss. What's all this talk about treasure?"

"Oh, it's just this silly story that's been exaggerated . . ." Taylor started, but the sound of forks hitting plates stopped her. She looked around and saw the angry faces of the people sitting around her.

"It is not a silly story. It our *history*."

"Hi, Millie. I didn't see you amongst this crowd. Thanks for your story and pointing out Grant's obvious showmanship in front of press row."

"No problem, but we will have a problem if you think Hung Island's Treasure Hunt is silly."

Taylor grimaced. How could she have forgotten PR 101? Don't upset the locals, especially if you're a nonlocal. "You know, Millie, it's probably because I've never heard the full story. All I know is something about the full moon being closest to the Earth. Why don't you tell us both so we can really get the feel of the legend."

"Of course! The history of Hung is so interesting. See, it all started in 1790 when pirates ruled this part of the ocean. Dashing pirates with big . . . swords." Millie grinned with excitement.

"Yes, a boat full of sexy pirates. I think we get that part," Taylor said as she tried not to laugh.

"But it was the pirate captain who was the sexiest of all with his long thick . . . brown hair and glowing emerald eyes," Millie continued with enthusiasm as she ignored the men rolling their eyes. "Anyway, they had been doing what pirates do—they got some booty. They had *a lot* of booty and were enjoying it quite a bit when the British navy tracked them down. It became a race that ended when the pirate captain found this small island. There were only a few settlers here and they thought they were under attack. So they hid the treasure because it was so big they didn't know what to do with it."

Trey choked on his iced tea. "I'm sorry. Just for clarification, what was so big?"

Millie gave him a look like he was dimwitted. "The ship, duh. So, the sexy pirate captain ran the ship ashore. His men quickly unloaded large trunks filled with jewels, liquor, gold, and then the women."

This time it was Taylor's cameraman who stopped her. "Wait. What women?"

Millie shook her head, disappointed. "Weren't you listening? I told you they were getting lots of booty. So, once all the treasure was unloaded and sitting on the beach, he ordered his men to come near. He looked up at the stars and the bright full moon that seemed so close he could reach out and touch it. He told them, 'On this night when t' full moon be so close, t' tides be at their lowest, we bury our treasure under her watchful eye.' So the men worked all night to bury the stolen treasure before the pirate captain sent them to every house in the small town. The pirate captain stood in the town square as his men, the wenches, and the settlers gathered as one. He told them the British were near and made a deal with them. If they hid his crew, his crew would always protect them and never do them any harm."

"So, what happened to them?" the cameraman asked.

"That day they worked feverishly building small huts around the island where the crew took their wenches and a spare settler or two. They pretended to be living there as the settlers when the British arrived that evening. The British stormed the island demanding the settlers to turn over the crew. The settlers said there was no crew. That only one man came off the boat last night—the pirate captain.

"The soldiers turned to where the pirate captain stood tall and proud in the town square overlooking the ocean. 'Where's the treasure?' the British demanded. The pirate captain just laughed as his green eyes glowed in the moonlight. The British captain pulled out a rope and threw it over the large nearby tree, which is now the site of Seawave Resort. Even after being beaten, the pirate captain still refused to tell where the treasure was buried. So the rope was placed around his neck and he was raised into the night sky. It's said his last words were, 'Aaarg, Davey Jones's locker is calling me home.' With a howl of pain that echoed in the night sky, he died on that very spot. One of the women settlers looked up at him and announced to the crowd, 'Wow, that man was hung!' And that's how the island became known as Hung Island." Millie crossed her arms and sat back in her chair with a flourish.

"That makes no sense. Why wouldn't the crew just go dig up the treasure?" The cameraman asked.

"Ah, because the British never left. And the crew followed their captain's orders and refused to leave the settlers unprotected. The crew and settlers kept their word and never told. It's even said that descendants of the crew are still here protecting the island today. So every year, when the moon is closest to the Earth and the tide is at its lowest point, the people, and now tourists, search for the buried treasure. It's said the person who finds it will have eternal life."

"Wait," Taylor interjected. "I heard it was the person who finds it will get the key to bring the pirate captain back."

"That's not it," one of the local fisherman said from his nearby table. "You'll be granted three wishes."

"No, Clyde. If you find the treasure you get . . ."

Taylor leaned closer to her cameraman. "Well, you get the picture now."

"Yeah, I do. Why aren't we filming that movie?"

"I don't do pirates, hung or otherwise," Taylor smiled innocently and turned back to Trey.

Trey shook his head. "Good thing I don't have to worry about that. Do you know how many men are dressed as pirates this week? But," he shrugged, "the story of Hung Island will be fun to tell our children someday. I know we aren't thinking of having kids right now, but you'll be the best mother. I can see you telling him stories every night."

"Her. I'm totally going to have a girl. And you'll be the overprotective daddy teaching her how real gentlemen should treat her. We may lead a very untraditional life, but I'd always hoped to settle into a more traditional family lifestyle. I find it all so romantic and comforting."

"We'll have our own traditions. We'll celebrate every Christmas in Keeneston. We'll have our mellow Monday dinner, movie night, and so many other little things that are just ours." Trey reached across the table and put his hand over hers. He loved her so much, but he just couldn't propose until it was perfect.

"I know it's silly, but when I was young I used to dream of a man asking my father's permission to marry me and being surrounded by everyone I cared about while getting married. It wouldn't be a big, fancy wedding like in the movies. Rather a hometown, casual, romantic event. Too bad by the time I was twelve, any idea of family was gone."

"But you have me now and we're family." Trey squeezed her hand and smiled. He had an idea.

Chapter Five

Trey grabbed some t-shirts, jeans, and cowboy boots and shoved them in his Vultures duffle bag. He scanned the room and looked for his royal blue Keeneston High School baseball cap. Finding it hanging in the closet, he slipped it over his dark blond hair and tried not to look Taylor in the eyes as she stepped out of the shower and slid on her robe.

"Hey, hon. I forgot to tell you, but tonight is an overnight with the guys. Team building or something like that. I'm sure Coach will have us doing some stupid trust exercises."

"Right," Taylor laughed as she toweled off her long hair. "More like you'll be eating pizza and gossiping."

"How many times do I have to tell you? Men don't gossip."

"You can say it until you're blue in the face and I won't believe you. You forget I hear you guys when you have poker night here. Slap on some sensible shoes and dye your hair white. You'd make a fine fourth Rose sister."

"You heard us out of context. Anyway, gosh knows what Coach has planned for us, so I don't know if I'll be able to answer the phone right away if you call. Sorry to do this on the weekend. I had been hoping we could do something together tonight." Trey slung his duffle bag over his shoulder and kept his eye fixed on her red painted toes.

Taylor sighed as she ran a brush through her hair. "It's okay. I didn't get a chance to tell you that we'll be shooting a night scene anyway. I'll be on set well into tomorrow morning. So I wouldn't be here anyway."

"Have fun trying to manage Grant and Melanie today," Trey finally moved closer to her and gave her a quick kiss.

Taylor rolled her eyes. "I swear, I've never been so glad to be behind the camera. He's bad enough, but then throw in Melanie who literally hurls herself in front of every camera she sees. It's enough to make me scream. She'd rather be in front of the media cameras than mine. The easiest way to eat up what little budget we have is to be behind in shooting. If Melanie doesn't start moving away from the media cameras and onto the set, then we're going to fall behind. We just can't afford to do that."

"You're not their costar anymore. You're their boss. Remember that. Don't let them walk over you just because they see you as the teenager they are accustomed to seeing on film." Trey rubbed her back and looked into the steely determination shining in her eyes. There was his girl.

"You're right. I'm going to go full *coach* on them. Maybe I'll pick up a whistle and order their little butts around the set. I do love it, though, all of it. Don't tell anyone, but I'm getting the itch again. I found myself mouthing the words yesterday. I'm not ready for acting again, but being behind the camera has definitely enflamed my love for the craft again."

"That's great!" Trey wrapped his arms around her and spun her around before letting her body slide down his as her toes touched the ground once again. "This time, if you step in front of the camera, it will be purely for the joy of it. It's the same feeling I get when I step out on the field.

Peace, excitement, and happiness rush through you because you're doing something you love. You'll know when the time is right."

"Exactly! I'm so glad you understand it. I'll know when it's time. I'm just so excited, my fear is starting to fade. Surprising since my parents showed up, but I guess I'm stronger than I thought. Speaking of renewed . . ."

Trey's eyes rolled back as Taylor's hand caressed his growing erection. Her towel dropped to the floor and Trey decided leaving could wait a little while longer. His hand moved to cup her breast as she leaned her head back, giving him access to her neck. He was going to take it slow and kiss every inch of her naked body. But then she popped the button to his jeans. Taylor's hand slid into his jeans and wrapped around his shaft and he lost all control.

Trey ripped his shirt off and with Taylor's help was kicking off his pants in record time. Taylor hooked her leg around his waist and Trey grabbed her other leg. With his two large hands cupping her bottom, he sat her on the counter allowing her to lean back as he stood in front of her. Leaning over to tease her nipple with his tongue, he pumped into her. The sounds of her moans were more than enough to make up for the late start.

Taylor smiled happily as she slipped into a pair of black linen slacks and a light blue silk shirt that matched her eyes. Trey had headed out after he, um, helped her get ready . . . twice. When the house went quiet and her breathing returned to normal, she decided she was going to take Trey's advice. She was going to stop acting like the stars' friend and start acting like their boss. The first step was dressing the part. She slipped on her wedge sandals and looked in the mirror with a smile of satisfaction. She was going to kick ass today. It didn't matter that she was only twenty-five. She had twenty years of experience in this industry — more than most of the people on set.

As she drove up to the Seawave Resort, she saw that the number of people standing at the metal barriers surrounding the set had grown. But she didn't worry as much as she had before. She saw Millie stomp the foot of a gossip blogger and laughed. Taylor headed straight for Millie, answered all her questions, and even posed for some pictures with Jim Peters before taking him aside to talk about today's scenes and the shot they were planning for tonight.

It felt good to jump into the business side of things once again and to learn how to set a scene from a master director like Jim. When Grant tried to pull her in for a kiss, she stopped him cold with just a look and ordered him to get ready. They were starting on time today and anyone not ready would be docked pay. She'd never seen him move so fast before.

"This is going to be a great day," Taylor stated.

"I think you're right," Jim smiled at her new assertiveness.

The afternoon sun warmed Trey's arm as it rested on the open window of his pick-up truck. It had taken eight hours, but he was almost there. Black four-board fences and rolling hills dotted with horses and cattle were leading him home. He drove his truck around a sharp corner on the country road and waved as he saw Betsy and William Ashton galloping in a field nearby.

He slowed to a near crawl when he came upon the huge

tractor driving down the road. The man waved and Trey moved to pass. He gave a honk and waved at Old Man Tabby driving the tractor. Soon more cars appeared as they honked their hellos as Main Street of Keeneston, Kentucky, came into view. Trees lined both sides of the street. Colorful historic buildings were freshly painted and American flags flew on every lamppost. It felt great to be home.

"Welcome home, Trey!"

"Hiya, Pam! How are the boys doing?" Trey called out through his open window.

"Doing great. Playing soccer for Transylvania. My oldest is a junior and playing on the varsity team. My youngest will be a freshman there this fall."

"Tell them I said hi," Trey shouted before moving toward the café. If he didn't stop to say hi, then he'd get a broom to the head and a spoon to the hand.

Miss Daisy Mae Rose smiled as she put a pitcher of tea on the small outdoor bistro table for Noodle, the deputy sheriff, and his wife, Dr. Emma. Their four-year-old daughter, Ava, sat at the table playing with a doll as her tight curls bounced.

"Lily Rae, Violet Fae, our boy is home!" Miss Daisy hollered through the screen door of the Blossom Café as she hurried toward his open window.

"You've done a nice job with your flowers this year, Miss Daisy." Trey saw the window boxes and the barrels of bright flowers overflowing their sides.

"Is everything alright? Aren't you in summer training? Where's Taylor? What's wrong?" Miss Lily asked all in one breath as she hurried from the café along with everyone who was inside.

Trey laughed and truly felt at home. These women took care of everyone in this town and he loved them as if they were his own grandmothers. "Everything is fine. Taylor is filming today. It's Saturday and I don't have practice. I wanted to see y'all and thought I'd come for a quick visit."

Miss Lily snorted and relaxed her grip on her broom. He had a feeling they knew the real reason he was here. "In that case, Cy is out on the farm today. Gemma's working on another book. It looks like Taylor may have a sequel if the movie does well."

"I could be here to see Will and Cade," Trey told them, thinking that he had to make sure he stopped by and saw Will Ashton and Cade Davies, his old high school football coaches.

"No one likes a fibber," Miss Violet said sweetly.

"I swear — y'all know why I'm here, don't you?"

"Of course we do," Miss Daisy shrugged.

"How?"

"It's a gift," Miss Lily said as her sisters nodded their white heads. No way were he and the rest of the guys on the team like them. Taylor was crazy. "Well, get to it. We'll see you later, young man. And welcome home." Miss Lily and her sisters turned with their heads pressed together. Trey pressed on the gas pedal. There was still a point one percent chance he could make it to Cy's farm before the Keeneston grapevine did.

Trey turned into Cy and Gemma's driveway and headed down the long road lined with Bradford Pear trees. Cattle grazed in the pasture to the left, and crops filled some of the property to the right. A couple of horses galloped in pastures ahead. The large, light yellow farmhouse slowly came into view with its sweeping covered porches and bright flowers.

Trey parked his truck and watched as Gemma Davies

unfolded herself from the large porch swing. Her hair was pulled back into a simple ponytail that swung as she put down her laptop and hurried down the wood steps toward him.

"Congratulations, Trey! You and Taylor will be so happy. And of course, you can have the wedding here at the farm if you wish. How does the second weekend in April sound as a wedding date?"

Trey was wrapped in a hug before he even had time to respond. "How?"

"The Keeneston phone tree was activated before you even pulled away from the café. Bets are being placed. With your football schedule, we've had to narrow it down to the actual day. So, second Saturday in April, right?" Gemma winked.

"I'll keep that in mind. So, Cy already knows why I'm here? Where is he?" Trey asked as he looked around the farmland.

"Nope. He's out riding with the girls." Gemma lifted her hand to shield the sun and squinted into the distance. "Oh, there they are. You may want to move to the side. This is their finish line."

"Finish?" Trey didn't get a chance to finish asking his question as Gemma pushed him aside.

He looked into the distance and saw three horses racing toward them. Cy led the group with his cowboy hat pulled low over his eyes. Two red-headed girls with long, wavy hair streaming behind them charged after him. One of the twins pulled ahead of Cy and Trey could hear her taunting her father and sister.

Her sister's face was set in determination at the taunt as she urged her horse faster. Cy's face was covered in a grin of pure enjoyment as he squeezed his thighs, sending his horse rocketing forward and past the twins. Hooves thundered down the dirt road as they galloped past Trey. The breeze caused dust to float up around him as he watched Cy cross the finish line first followed by the twins.

"Aw, Dad," seven-year-old Reagan and Riley both whined at the same time.

"Sorry, girls. Your old man still has it. You'll just have to wait for another day to beat me," Cy laughed as he swung his leg over the saddle and hopped to the ground. "Trey! What's going on?"

"Trey!" The girls squealed as they slid from their horses and raced to wrap their arms around his waist.

Trey laughed as he ruffled his hands in their hair. Both girls looked up with shining hazel eyes and starting talking at once.

"Then Gabe threw dirt at me."

"But Zain didn't."

"So we waited until he thought he was alone."

"And made him a mud pie."

"And whoops, we dropped it from the tree . . ."

"And it just happened to land all over him."

"Zain saw us, but didn't tell Mr. Mo or Miss Dani about it."

"He's not a tattler."

"But you know who is?" Both girls turned and looked at each other before looking back up at Trey.

"Who?" Trey asked as he tried to find the small mole on the side of Reagan's mouth. It was the only way to tell them apart.

"Our cousin Dylan. He totally told on us when we went playing down at Aunt Paige's special place when we were supposed to be helping Nana and Papa."

"Little boys can be like that."

The girls rolled their eyes at his statement. "Boys are stupid," they said in unison.

"That they are," Cy chuckled as he closed the gate to the pasture where the horses had been put after they were unsaddled. "So, to what do I owe the unexpected pleasure of seeing you?"

"I was hoping to have a word with you in private." Trey looked down and didn't miss the exchange between the twins. He had a feeling nothing was ever private around the house. The girls had inherited their father's spying abilities and their mother's nose for gossip.

"Sure, come on in. Gem, can you watch the girls for a minute?"

"Of course. Come on, girls. Playtime is over. Time to feed the animals."

"Aw, Mom . . ."

"Nope, that whining may work on your father, but it doesn't on me. Off with you two." Gemma tried to sound serious, but Trey heard the laughter in her voice as he followed Cy into the house.

"So, what's going on?" Cy asked as he grabbed a beer from the fridge and passed it to Trey.

"You know Taylor and I have been together for a long time now. I still have trouble believing she wants me, but after all this time I guess I'm finally ready to admit she actually wants to be with me. It's funny. I would come home from practice and always expect her to be gone. I was waiting for her to realize she could do so much better than me." Trey looked blindly down at his beer as he held it in his hands.

"That's the sign of having a good woman. Gosh knows why they stay, but you love them even more for it. So, you're finally ready to make an honest woman out of

Taylor, huh?" Cy twisted off the cap to his beer and took a drink.

"I am, but beneath her edgy personality lies a traditional woman. She told me she always dreamed of a man asking her father's permission to marry and then her father walking her down the aisle. Well, I had the honor of meeting her father this week and now understand why that dream of hers died."

Cy put his beer down hard on the counter. "You met her father?"

"Father and mother. They were horrible. They came storming into the house right when I was about to propose and demanded that I leave their daughter alone. Taylor came home and the look on her face was heartbreaking. All they wanted was to be her manager again, for twelve percent. Oh, and to have her marry Grant instead of me and be his manager too." Trey took a deep drink of his beer as he tried to keep his calm.

Cy didn't bother trying. He slammed his hand hard against the countertop. Glasses in the cabinet rattled and his hazel eyes turned to stone.

"You have to protect her. They are dangerous. Her mother and father used to abuse her both mentally and physically. They are constantly high on drugs and looking for their next fix of cocaine or the spotlight. They'll take either and in the process will use anyone to get it, not caring who they hurt along the way."

Trey nodded. Taylor had told him all about her parents when they were in college. But hearing it was different from seeing it. "I will. It's the reason I'm here. In reality, you're more of a father to her than anyone else. It's you she calls every week. It's you who helped her get a place to live, taught her to cook, and how to drive. It was you who helped her get ready for her first date and who met the guy at the door. It was you who helped her get her GED and who attended her college graduation. And it's you we spend the holidays with. So, it's you I feel I should ask for permission to marry Taylor."

Trey took a gulp and watched as Cy took a calming breath before a smile broke out on his face. "Well, you have it, son." Cy held out his hand and Trey shook it with relief. He hadn't realized he had been so nervous.

The screen door was thrown open as Gemma, the twins, and the Rose sisters all tumbled in. "About time, young man! Now, what do you think of the first weekend in May?" Miss Lily asked.

Chapter Six

"Take it from me. A lady likes a man with a little bad boy to him." Henry Rooney, a Keeneston defense lawyer, winked.

Neely Grace Rooney, his wife and law partner, rolled her eyes as she bounced their three-year-old daughter, Addison, on her hip. "You know better than to listen to him, right?"

Trey laughed as Henry looked wounded before looking back at Trey and giving him a smirk. "It worked, didn't it? I got the most beautiful and classy woman in the entire town to marry me. Now, come here, precious. Let Daddy protect you from all those bad boys."

Henry took their daughter from Neely and headed to where the little girls were shaking their heads in bafflement at the boys down in the yard throwing dirt at each other.

"Congratulations to you and Taylor. We won't breathe a word of it until she calls to tell us the news herself. Oh, there's Chrystal and Dinky with little Landon. Last play date, Landon kissed Addison and I thought Henry was going to blow a gasket." Neely Grace hurried away to calm Henry who was trying to protectively keep Addison behind him as Landon toddled over.

"This will be you someday. I can't believe it. It makes me feel old," Will Ashton joked as he and his wife,

McKenna, approached.

"After a couple years in the NFL, I already feel old. I don't know how you did it for so long," Trey said with wonder. Will had been a very successful quarterback in the NFL for almost a decade. Further, he came back to Keeneston and took up coaching the high school team that Trey had played on along with Coach Cade Davies.

"You thinking of coming home? I could use a running back coach," Will smiled at him.

"Not yet. But I think that's our plan. When we're ready to have kids, we'll move back here." Trey and Taylor had already discussed it. There were advantages they could give their kids with their NFL and Hollywood connections. But they both agreed that when it came to raising them, it was better to raise them in a place like Keeneston.

Mo and Dani's car pulled up and their twin eight-year-old boys, Zain and Gabe, leapt out and dashed to where the other boys were playing. Sienna and Carter, Will and Kenna's children, quickly got everyone's attention as Sienna tossed a football back and forth with her brother.

"Wow, she's got an arm on her," Trey said with wonder as Sienna threw a bullet at her brother.

"Yup. She got her mother's fashion sense and my arm. At ten, she's now old enough to really be competitive. She's the quarterback for the local flag football team. And Carter, three years younger, is dying to be old enough to play. But he has no interest in throwing the ball. He likes catching and running with it." Will watched his kids as Sienna organized the older kids into teams.

"Do you think he wants to play in the NFL?" Trey asked as he watched Sienna throw a zinger to her brother.

"Nope. He wants to race horses. We don't really care what he does, as long as he's happy. Now Sienna lives and breathes football, but she's only ten. They have lots of time to grow up and decide what they want to do in life. Gosh knows she argues like her mother, so I wouldn't rule out her being a lawyer either."

Trey watched the kids play a little more and then couldn't help but cringe as Sophie, Annie and Cade Davies's nine-year-old daughter, landed a huge hit on Gabe.

"Nice hit, huh?" Annie asked as she and Cade approached, Cade shaking his head.

"I can't get her to stop. *Someone* enjoys teaching her takedowns. Welcome back and congratulations." Cade pulled him in for a quick hug and a pat on the back.

"Thanks, Coach."

"I think you can call me Cade now. I haven't been your coach in years."

Trey couldn't do it, though. No matter how many years passed, he and Will would always be "Coach" to him. They settled down and talked football, Taylor, and the movie before Paige and Cole joined them. Their sons, Ryan, nine, and Jackson, six, ran off to play football with the group after saying their congratulations.

"I have some clothes and things for you to take to Taylor after you pop the question. She had wanted them for the movie," Paige told him as she rolled her eyes at Ryan blowing a kiss at Sienna. "I swear, Cole. Your son is going to be shot and I wouldn't blame Will for doing it."

"I'll go talk to him, again," Cole sighed as Dani and Mo walked up to offer their congratulations.

"Do you think you'll get married here?" Dani asked.

"Dear, don't you think he should be allowed to propose first?" Mo asked sweetly.

"They've been together seven years; it's hardly a

surprise and I'm sure they've already discussed it."

"Oh, they have. And I know it'll be here," Gemma called out from across the porch where she sat with the Rose sisters.

John Wolfe lumbered up the steps and shook Trey's hand. "First week of April is lovely," he said before taking a seat next to his girlfriend, Miss Lily.

"If it's the second week in May, the sheriff's office will be happy to help with keeping the gossips, including my lovely sister-in-law, away," Marshall Davies joked as he and his wife, Katelyn, made their way up the steps.

"I heard that!" Gemma laughed.

"Mr. Everett, can I be a flower girl?" eight-year-old Sydney asked. Marshall and Katelyn's six-year-old son, Wyatt, already had run off to join his cousin Jackson.

"I want to be one too!" seven-year-old Layne and Piper called as they ran over.

"Pleeeeeeease?" they all begged.

Trey laughed as Miles and Morgan whispered to Layne that it wasn't polite to request to be in someone else's wedding. Similarly, Tammy and Pierce informed Piper of that fact as their four-year-old son, Dylan, struggled to get down so he could play with his friends.

"It's okay," Trey smiled at the three pairs of matching hazel eyes. The cousins looked nothing alike except for those eyes. "I'll talk to the boss about it after she agrees to marry me and see what I can do."

The girls' faces lit with excitement as they headed off to practice being flower girls and Trey got updates on how everyone was doing. Miles's farming company was expanding. Morgan's consulting firm was growing to include public relations, including helping Taylor out with promotion for her movie. Katelyn was getting ready to hire a new vet at the animal hospital. Tammy was happily running Rooney & Rooney since Kenna had left to become the county's prosecutor.

"Thank goodness when Kenna left, Neely Grace was there to fill the void. I don't know how I've kept from shooting Henry and those horrible pick-up lines. I think he feels he has to use them all on me since Neely gets mad when he uses them on her," Tammy told him. He could believe it, but Henry wouldn't be Henry unless he acted just a little sleazy.

"And how's the Cropbot doing?" Trey asked Pierce about his farming invention.

"Doing great. We sell out every year and are upping production. Soon we're going to outgrow the facility we're in and will have to find a new one," Pierce told him. It was hard to imagine that these two dressed in jeans and cowboy boots were millionaires or that Dani and Mo were royalty of the small Middle Eastern nation of Rahmi. It was one of the wonderful things about Keeneston—everyone could be themselves and be treated as such.

Soon the Rose sisters, along with Marcy Davies and Betsy Ashton, started setting out food. Almost naturally, the men, women, and children separated into their respective corners. The women sat on the porch telling stories while the kids sat on the lawn under a large maple tree. The men moved to the stairs as they balanced plates of food on their knees.

"Have you thought of a special way to propose?" Mo asked as he took a bite of fried chicken.

"Not yet. It has to be super romantic, though. Taylor deserves a perfect proposal."

"I think you'll find that as long as it comes from you, it will be perfect," Miles informed him in such a serious way it seemed the complete opposite of the romantic words he said.

"So says the man who painted a water tower to ask his wife to marry him," Cy teased.

"Oh, and riding into town on a horse was what? Just convenient?" Marshall teased his brother Cy. "Why don't you just ask her? I asked Katelyn at home. It was private and completely ours."

"And completely boring," Cade laughed before turning to Trey. "You know how I proposed to Annie—on the field after the championship game. You could do something like that at the Vultures field. You could do it two ways: at the first game in front of everyone or have a romantic night out and end up on the field all alone."

"No woman can resist a man on a horse. I'm just sayin'," Cy put in as the debate of best marriage proposal raged on.

Taylor gripped her coffee mug tightly and took a deep breath. It was two in the morning and they'd been filming since ten the previous morning. If Melanie didn't hit her mark, then Taylor was going to kill her. This was the twenty-eighth take and it was so easy Cyndi Lu, the friendly stalker, could do it.

Jim was yelling at Melanie. Grant was on his cell phone probably doing a live play-by-play via social media. The cameramen were yawning and the boom mic was dipping dangerously close to Melanie's head as she yelled back at Jim. It was a nightmare, to say the least. But they had to get this scene done tonight or they'd fall behind in production. With the chance of rain in the forecast, she didn't want to risk pushing it off for another week.

Taylor slammed down her coffee mug and drew everyone's attention. The cameramen were startled, the boom mic shot back into the air, and Jim and Melanie stopped yelling. Even Grant looked up from his cell phone.

"Jim, go direct. Gentlemen, get ready to film. Grant, get in position," Taylor ordered in a voice just short of a yell.

She grabbed Melanie by the arm and half-dragged the starlet down to the nearby ocean. "This is when you see Darin for the first time since receiving the flowers he sent you. You're standing in the waves and look up at the gazebo lit up with lights mixed between the flowers. You see him standing there with flowers in his hand. You run to him. Despite only knowing your first name, he's somehow tracked you down across the state to tell you he loves you. You run to him and then stop where the big X is on the grass about five feet from him," Taylor called over her shoulder as she took off in an excited run.

Emotion of the scene filled her eyes and face conveying the shock, excitement, and love Kathy felt for Darin. Taylor slowed as she approached the X. "Darin?" She whispered as if she was seeing a ghost. She stopped at the X and waited for Grant to say his line.

Instead of Grant's line, the sound of creaking metal ruined the moment just as the lights overhead used to cast the soft romantic glow broke loose. Taylor only spared a quick look at the lights about to crash down on her head before leaping forward. At the same time, Grant had started rushing toward her as the lights smashed into the ground right where Taylor had been standing. She jumped into Grant's arms and cried out as a piece of glass sliced into her leg, but was otherwise unhurt.

"Taylor!" Jim called as he ran forward issuing orders.

She heard Melanie crying hysterically how she was almost killed–*she* as in Melanie, not Taylor. Grant yelled at Melanie to shut up as he pulled Taylor all the way into his arms.

"It's okay. You're safe now," Grant whispered against her hair and held her tightly as she began to shake. "Let me see the cut, babe."

Taylor finally looked down and saw the blood pooling around the shard of glass sticking out of her calf. "Oh crap. That's gonna hurt when it's pulled out." She laid her head against Grant's broad, make-up-bronzed chest and closed her eyes.

Paramedics and the on-set doctor rushed in followed by Millie and Cyndi Lu staring from the driveway of the resort. Grant held her hand as the shard of glass was removed and the area cleaned and closed with four stitches.

"It's all over," Grant said soothingly. Taylor opened her eyes and saw Millie and Cyndi Lu looking worriedly over at her. Melanie was in front of Millie waving her arms and telling how she almost died while Jim stood over Taylor looking worried. "Come on, I'll take you home," Grant offered.

Taylor nodded and stood up before she thanked the doctor. "I'm okay, really. I'm sorry I sort of shut off there for a moment. But, I'm alright now."

"No," Jim cut in seriously. "Let Grant take you home while I look into this."

Taylor looked over at Grant and gave him a nod of her head. "Okay for tonight only. Let's get the set back in order ASAP and keep our fingers crossed we can film tomorrow night."

Heat and pressure pulsed on her leg where her stitches were. She hissed in discomfort and was surprised when

Grant hurried to put his arm around her and help her toward his rented Porsche.

"Taylor, are you okay? Is there any truth that someone is trying to kill Melanie?" Millie called out.

"Come on, not tonight," Grant shot back, annoyed at the questions.

Taylor was shocked. She thought for sure Grant would be in front of the camera retelling his heroics over and over again. Magnifying her shock was the fact his hands were staying in respectable locations as well. "I'm fine, Millie. Thank you. And no, no one is trying to kill anyone."

"Miss Jefferies! Watch out for him. I may not think Trey Everett is good enough for you, but Grant Elliott is a pig," Cyndi Lu screamed in warning.

"Oink-oink, babe."

"Really, Grant?" Taylor rolled her eyes as he helped her into his car. "I was almost thinking you were a decent guy."

Grant shut the door and strolled to his side. "Never think that, babe. I'm not a decent guy. I'll do anything to keep climbing in this industry."

"Even suck up to the producer? You may fool others, but I think you're a nice guy under all that oil," Taylor teased as he drove her the short distance home.

"Come on. I'll help you inside. Then I can exploit the fact I was in your house while Trey was gone."

Taylor shook her head in sympathy. It must be hard to be Grant. It must be exhausting. She saw how much he worked out. She hated to say it, but it was a shallow industry and one of the reasons she hired him was because he looked the part of a Hollywood heartthrob.

"Go on. It's your reward for being so kind to me tonight."

Grant stopped in surprise as he helped her to the couch

in her living room. "Yeah, and then one of the top running backs in the league will be having a private talk with me. Geez, Taylor. This place is so . . . un-Hollywood."

"I think *homey* is the word you're looking for." Taylor looked around at the pictures of their friends and the couple over the years. The warm colors and the cozy furniture made the room feel snuggly. Definitely not something you'd imagine after seeing celebrity homes on television.

The normalcy was broken as the front door flung open. Grant turned and blocked her view, but the fake crying told her instantly who it was.

"Oh, baby. My baaaaaby! Don't worry, Mama's here."

The pain Taylor felt in her leg was nothing compared to the anger that managed to push her shaky nerves away. Taylor shot up and wobbled only slightly. Grant steadied her and she advanced on her parents.

"I told you I never wanted to see you again. I told you were no longer welcome anywhere near me. By what right do you think you can just walk into my house?" she asked in a deadly voice.

"But, baby, you took our advice. You're here with Grant instead of Trey. And when we heard that you were hurt on set, we had to see you. We've already worked up an angle to spin it in order to get you and Grant tons of press," her mother said sweetly as if the last ten years just hadn't happened.

"As great as that sounds, I'm out. I don't do parents." Grant wedged himself out the door and hurried to his car as her father turned to chase after him, trying to pitch them as his managers.

Taylor limped to the open door as her mother continued talking about press conferences and how they'd handle everything. "Here, just sign this managing contract and we can start right now."

"Get out of my house," Taylor said softly as she hobbled out to the front porch. Neighbors started to file out of their homes as her father's pitch to Grant rang through the night.

"And look, you'll see we already gave you the discounted price of twelve percent," her mother was saying.

"Enough!" Taylor screamed at the top of her lungs. Her parents' eyes went wide in momentary shock. Grant took advantage of the opportunity and leapt into his car. The sound of his tires spinning on the sandy driveway was the only sound beside the ocean waves in the night air.

"That is no way to speak to your mother, young lady," her father said in a way that brought to Taylor's mind a flashback of him pulling off his belt when she was thirteen. But she wasn't thirteen anymore.

"You may have brought me into this world, but I stopped having a mother and father a long time ago. I will call the sheriff if you're not out of here by the time I count to five." Taylor pulled out her cell phone and pushed 9-1-1 onto the keyboard. "I told you last time, I never want to see you again. Now get the hell off my property!" Taylor yelled, losing all her patience.

"This isn't over!" her mother shot back as her father hurried them into the car.

"Yes, it is. It was over when the judge signed the order all those years ago." Taylor put her phone away as they drove off into the night. Her nerves were frayed and the sound of clapping only pissed her off more.

"Did you enjoy the show?" Taylor snipped.

A sexy woman grinned from where she stood on the beach with a great pair of heels dangling from her fingertips. Her dark brown hair shone in the moonlight and her hazel eyes seemed to sparkle.

"Sure did. All this time I thought you were some helpless, ditzy blonde. Who knew? But, you go, girl is all I have to say. I might actually go see one of your movies now." She flashed a smile and Taylor relaxed against her door and returned the smile before the woman sauntered off down the beach. The stranger's praise boosted her spirits. She was woman and everyone had just heard her roar.

Taylor limped back inside and changed into her pajamas. She pushed open the window so she could listen to the waves and crawled under the covers. Tomorrow was a new day and she wanted to make the most of it. Her mind was already rearranging the shooting schedule to get them back on track when she drifted off to sleep.

Chapter Seven

Trey drove past the stadium with purpose. He had a plan for the most romantic proposal. He drove across Captain's Bridge and stopped at the "Welcome to Hung Island" sign. He pulled out his cell phone and snapped a picture of him next to the sign.

Can't wait to be home with you, he texted to Taylor. He hopped back in the car and headed to their favorite restaurant.

He ordered her favorite meal and snapped a picture of the food when it arrived. *Bringing my love her favorite dinner.* He hurried to the car and planned out the rest of the pictures. When he was close to home, he stopped and took a picture of himself on the beach. *Can't wait to spend every night with you on our beach.* The next picture would be of him in their living room down on one knee. Trey planned on asking Taylor to get the dinners set out while he snapped the picture and sent it to her phone. Taylor would get it while in the kitchen and then come out and see him on one knee.

As he pulled up, the nervous energy nearly made him crash into the house. "Taylor?" he called out. But there was no answer. He stepped further into the house. "Did you get my pictures?"

A pillow launched through the door and hit him on the

face. "Your pictures? You bet I got your pictures. I can't escape your damn pictures and here you come acting all innocent," Taylor cried.

"I thought you'd like them. I thought they were sweet. I'm sorry they upset you." Trey's shoulders slumped. Where did he go wrong?

"You think pictures of you with your face in some stripper's tits is sweet?"

Trey paused in his thinking. "What? Strippers?"

"You got that innocent act down pat and here I thought I was the actor in the family. So, this is the male bonding you were doing with the guys? Too bad someone decided to take pictures and now they're all over the internet and entertainment television. Grant's been shoving them in my face all day. Cyndi Lu's been telling me to leave your cheating ass. And after last night, it's just too much for me to handle."

Taylor walked over to the table and set her tablet down in front of him. Why was she limping? What was she talking about? Trey looked down at the tablet and cringed. Filling the screen was a photo of his head buried between two very large glittery breasts.

"This may be a picture of me, but it's fake. I wasn't at a strip club. And what happened last night?"

"There was an accident on set. Some lights fell and I had to jump out of the way. A piece of glass cut me. Don't worry, while you were *bonding,* Grant took care of me until my parents showed up again." Taylor moved her hands to her hips and Trey knew she was getting fired up.

"Why didn't you call me? I would have come home," he said as gently as possible.

"I don't think you could have heard me with those earmuffs on."

"Really, Taylor? After all this time and all the media attention, you think I would do something like this? Here," Trey picked up his bag and dumped it on the table. "Not a single speck of glitter to be found. And look, that's the shirt I ruined when I stained the deck. I threw it out three months ago. The photo is fixed and you should have enough trust in me to know that. I believed you when there were pictures everywhere on the news of Grant slapping your butt, and that actually happened. This didn't happen." Now it was Trey's time to put his hands on his hips as Taylor's shoulders sagged before she collapsed onto the couch.

"I'm sorry. I don't know what's come over me. Deep down I knew better, but after everything that happened last night and the fact I hardly slept . . . I just overacted. I didn't even think to look at it beneath the surface."

Trey sat down next to her and tucked her against his chest. "It's okay. We knew the gossips would be coming after us when you stepped back into the limelight. And it's fine because I know I can trust you. We don't need to even look at these. We haven't for years; let's not start now."

"I trust you too. I'm so sorry I just forgot for a moment. You're the best man I know and you'd never do anything to hurt me like that."

Taylor leaned forward and kissed him. Her fingers trailed down his chest and her hand spread over his abdomen. In an instant, the kiss went from asking for forgiveness to demanding. Trey didn't complain at all. He knew the pressures of being in the public life. She got up, peeled off her shirt, and began hooking her finger in a come hither motion. He no longer gave a damn about Grant, her parents, or the gossips. And when her hand appeared from behind the bedroom door and dropped her bra to the floor, he forgot all about everything except Taylor.

Trey slowly moved Taylor's arm from his chest. After they made love, she fell asleep in his arms and was now curled around him. It took a long time, but he finally got untangled from her arms and legs. Slowly, he pushed the covers aside and stole out of bed.

The moon was almost full and the light allowed him to see easily into the living room. He bent down and picked his pants off the floor. Digging into his pocket, he pulled out the jewelry box and sighed. Another perfect proposal down the drain. He opened the box and stared at the moonlight reflecting off the diamond. Frustration welled inside of him. He'd give her the perfect proposal, even if it killed him.

The motion light flicked on out front and light filled the room. The sound of something hitting the front door had him running down the hall and throwing open the door. A streak of orange pigtails was all he saw of the woman running away. Looking down, he saw the picture of him at the strip club on the stoop. Written in red marker was *You don't deserve her.*

Taylor woke up early. Her leg was thrown over Trey's much thicker one and her head nestled against his chest. She felt fantastic. And she felt horrible. Sleeping through the night made a ton of difference on her outlook, but then she realized how badly she'd treated Trey the night before. He was too good for her. He put up with her accusations and calmly proved them wrong, all the while forgiving her the second she said she was sorry. The result: she felt miserable and had no idea how to make it up to him. Taylor crawled out of bed and slipped into her light blue silk robe before heading for the kitchen. The least she could do was make him breakfast.

The bacon was cooked and she was just finishing the scrambled eggs when a sleepy Trey made his way into the kitchen. Taylor poured him a cup of coffee and he quickly perked up after a few sips.

"What is all this?" he asked as he snagged a piece of bacon from the plate.

"My apology. I'm so embarrassed for the way I acted last night."

"There's nothing to apologize for. We both know living a public life is hard, just like when I have to watch you kiss someone on screen. But I know it's not real."

"I know, and that's why I'm so sorry. You've never made me feel bad about the tabloids. Even last week when they said I was pregnant with Grant's child because they snapped a picture of me on set with him after I ate a hamburger." Trey stared her down with a smile playing on his lips. "Okay, and a double scoop hot fudge sundae and a beer or two. It's Melanie's fault. Her constant demands have caused me to gain ten pounds."

Trey laughed and she felt the embarrassment fade away. He always made her a better person. He'd called her out, but then he'd forgiven her just as fast.

"Fine, laugh it up. No one is saying you look pregnant."

"I'd hope not or we'd have to have a serious discussion." Trey bent down and kissed her as he sneaked another piece of bacon. "What do you have planned today?"

"I'm hoping to be on set in an hour. It shouldn't be a

late night, though. I think we're planning the reshoot for tomorrow night, depending on the weather."

"Good. Then I'll have you for the whole night."

Trey finished breakfast while Taylor got ready for work. He picked up the paper and read the story about Taylor's accident on set and grimaced at the picture of Grant holding her. He hadn't lied. He did trust her, but that didn't mean he trusted Grant. He flipped the paper over so he wouldn't have to see the picture and looked down at an article about a carnival being in town.

He'd forgotten about that. It was set up near the stadium and he'd seen it driving to practice. That was it! They had that huge Ferris wheel set up overlooking the bay and Hung Island. He could propose there! With renewed enthusiasm, Trey started planning.

Chapter Eight

"For crying out loud, Melanie," Jim cursed. "Did you suddenly forget you're an actress?"

Melanie stomped her foot and crossed her arms over her fake chest. "I just don't get the emotion of the script."

"The emotion?" Jim yelled. The question hung heavy in the ballroom they had converted to a 1960s diner to cut down on the cost of having to move everything and everyone to yet another location. The exterior shots had been taken last month in Las Vegas.

"She just met the guy. Why would she care if she never saw him again?" Melanie pouted.

"The dance we filmed showed the connection blooming. It's as if it's right in front of you. You just can't reach it and that tears at your heart. Just like the fact you'll never get an Oscar. Let's do it again!"

Taylor hid her smile as she watched everyone hurry to their places. Melanie's face was red with anger. But Jim was right. Melanie was flat and this was a very emotional moment. This was the scene when Darin and Kathy realized their interest in each other but have to leave not knowing if they'll ever see each other again.

"CUT!" Taylor grimaced as Jim threw his clipboard across the room. "I can't take it! Go home. And Melanie, if you can't give me some semblance of emotion, I will take every pair of shoes you have and set them on fire. Now that ought to get some emotion out of you. And don't think I won't do it."

"Wow, and I thought Coach was tough."

Taylor jumped as she heard Trey's whispered words. "You scared me to death," she said as she grew embarrassed that she'd been caught so unaware.

"I thought we could go out on a date."

"Better not let her drink since she's got my bun in her oven," Grant swaggered over and grinned as if it were true.

But Trey just rocked back on his cowboy boots and smiled like a cat that just ate the canary. If women could see Grant and Trey side by side, they would name a new Sexiest Man of the Year. Grant's tan was courtesy of his make-up artist and his teeth were just a shade from blinding. He was tall but a couple of inches shorter than Trey. He was muscular, but it seemed like an illusion compared to Trey's build. And Grant was always sure to lose his shirt in a split second. While nice to look at it, it didn't compare to Trey's look: the understated jeans that hugged all the right places and the t-shirt gently stretched over a broad chest, hanging just slightly loose around Trey's tapered waist. It all left you wondering what was beneath the clothing. And one couldn't ignore Grant's strutting peacock attitude compared to the gentlemanly manners that left a woman feeling respected and out of breath all at once.

"I wouldn't worry about anyone believing that. After all, I just saw an article saying you have a secret lover," Trey continued to grin and Taylor wondered what was up.

"It's the price you pay for being so good-looking. I'm everyone's lover. As long as I leave them satisfied, then I've done my job. Right, babe?" Taylor rolled her eyes as Grant preened.

"Well, he seems like a nice guy. I'm glad you're happy with him. The picture of you two online is adorable. Well, ready to go, Taylor?" Trey asked as if he hadn't just dropped a bomb on Grant.

"Wait, him? What you talking about?" Grant was already pulling out his phone and turning it on. "Holy hell." Grant was on the phone and yelling at his agent in the blink of an eye.

Taylor looked at Trey and back to where Grant was running from the set. "I don't even want to know."

"He doesn't matter to us. I have something great planned for tonight."

"Sounds fun. Let me get my stuff out of the trailer and we can head out. What are we doing?"

"Going to the carnival. It has a huge Ferris wheel overlooking the ocean and Hung Island. And I can probably even win you a stuffed animal if you'd like."

"A big pink bear?" Taylor teased as they stepped into her trailer.

"Anything my lady desires. Including funnel cakes, cotton candy, and lemon shake-ups. We'll do the whole shebang."

"Oh my gosh, that sounds so good." Taylor picked up her purse, "Okay, let's go! I can't wait to go on some of the rides."

Trey grabbed the door handle of the trailer but nothing happened. He pulled it again, but the door only rattled. "Is there a trick to opening the door?"

"No. It's just a door handle." Taylor paused and then took a sniff of the air. "Do you smell smoke?"

Trey breathed in. "Yes, and lots of it." He tried the door

with urgency, but it wouldn't budge.

Taylor turned to the back of the trailer and gasped. Through the window she saw flames. "Trey!"

Trey grabbed the handle again but pulled back quickly. "Damn, it's hot." He rushed to the front of the trailer and looked out the window. "There's fire all around us."

Taylor leapt onto the kitchen table and threw open the blinds. "No fire here, but the window only vents. It doesn't open. We can't get out."

Trey reached up and pulled her off the table as if he was moving a book. He flung open the overhead cabinets and ripped off the blinds. Grabbing hold of the bottom of the cabinet, he pulled back his legs and swung forward. The glass shattered on the impact and smoke rushed inside the trailer as the fire spread around them. A few more kicks and the window was mostly gone.

"The fire's spreading. Grab the doormat," Trey ordered as he used his boot to knock some hanging pieces of glass down.

Taylor rushed to grab the mat and threw it to him. Trey laid it over the broken glass and reached his hand out to help her step onto the table. "I'll go out first and drop down. I want you to carefully come out feet first and just drop. I'll catch you."

Trey wedged himself through the window. Taylor could see the glass ripping his shirt as his shoulder got stuck. He pushed through and disappeared from view. The trailer was getting hot now and the smoke was making it hard to see. She crawled along the table and looked out the window. Trey was looking nervously at the fire licking the underside of the trailer.

"Sweetheart, now is not the time to be fashionably late."

Taylor gave a quick nod and pushed her feet out the

window. The broken glass crunched under the mat as she scooted farther out. Closing her eyes tight, she pushed herself out. She fell for only a split second and then Trey's arms were around her. With a flick of his arm, he was cradling her and taking off at a dead run.

"You can put me down," Taylor tried to say jokingly but wound up coughing instead.

Trey only held her tighter and ran faster. There was a creaking sound of metal melting and then a whoosh of a fireball. Taylor's eyes went wide as she looked over Trey's shoulder and saw her trailer explode. Trey leapt forward and tucked her beneath him. They hit the ground hard as metal rained down around them.

Trey kept his arm around Taylor as they waited for Sheriff Wilson to talk to them. Jim stood on the other side of Taylor. Even Grant and Melanie had shown up to see what was going on.

The sheriff nodded his head and shook hands with the fire marshal before heading their way. "Mr. Everett, Miss Jefferies, have the paramedics checked you out yet?"

"Yes. I'm okay and Trey just had a minor cut on his shoulder," Taylor told him.

"What caused the fire, sheriff?" Trey asked.

Sheriff Wilson ran his hand through his hair and grimaced. "It appears one of the grounds crew was on a golf cart that had a can of gas on the back of it. It seems the gas can fell over when he was about ten feet from your trailer, causing gas to pour out as he drove past. We found the cart and the can. It matches up with the residue we found on the ground."

"So it was just a freak accident?" Taylor asked, sounding both relieved and disbelieving at the same time.

"I want to know if either of you recognizes anyone in these pictures." Sheriff Wilson held up three pictures and Taylor nodded.

"I know all of them. They all work here at the resort. That's Bubs, Mutt, and Gopher."

"Would any of them have a reason to hurt you?" Sheriff Wilson asked as he kept holding the pictures for her to see.

"Goodness, no. Bubs always leaves fresh flowers in my trailer. He's the head of the garden on the grounds. His wife just had their second boy and I was even invited to the christening. Mutt's a great guy. He's always puttering down at the marina and taught Trey how to sail. And Gopher? He takes care of the golf course. I don't know him all that well since I don't play golf. But we've worked together on charity golf scrambles and he seems like a nice guy. Why?"

"It was Bubs driving the cart. He said the same thing as you did, but I needed to make sure it was two-sided and not a delusional fan issue. So far it's looking like an accident. Go home and get some rest. I'll let you know whenever we get any more information."

Trey and Taylor shook the sheriff's hand and watched him stop to talk with his brother, who was also a deputy. The brother was currently giving her the once-over. She rolled her eyes. He was known for being a hound dog.

"Come on, sweetheart. Let's get home and clean up." Trey's hand rested on her lower back with gentle pressure to lead her toward his car.

"I'm sorry your date night was ruined. It sounded wonderful. I hope they're here a little longer. I've never been to a carnival before. As a kid, I was afraid of clowns and when I was a little older, my parents had me working all the time."

"Well, we will just have to try again. And I'll protect you from any wayward clowns," Trey grinned as he looked down at her.

Taylor smiled back, but then her stomach rumbled loud enough that Trey heard it.

"Well, it may not be the carnival, but let's go to the diner and get a big greasy burger and some beers."

"Right now, that's the most romantic thing I've heard all day." Taylor laced her fingers with his and batted her eyelashes as they both dissolved into laughter.

To say Trey was disappointed, upset, and worried was an understatement. But he tried to relax as he watched Taylor bite into the double bacon cheeseburger and wash it down with a beer. She looked so happy as she savored every bite. However, no matter how he tried to relax, the feeling that the other shoe was about to drop plagued him.

"This is so good," Taylor said for the fourth time before taking a fry and dipping it in some ranch dressing. "Casey, you're the best. You've made a great night out of a horrible one."

Casey actually blushed slightly from behind the soda fountain.

Trey pulled out his cell phone and skimmed the page. "We do have some good news, though. Tomorrow is the carnival's last night. You'll get to go after all."

"That's fantastic." Taylor paused to take another bite of her burger.

Trey was going to agree when two shadows fell over

Taylor, causing him to look up. The other shoe had just dropped. Looming behind Taylor and shooting daggers at him were none other than her parents.

"My baaaaby!" her mother wailed, causing the diner to fall silent and stare at their table.

Taylor's face went white and quickly to red to show her anger. Her hands started shaking as her mother wrapped her arms around her in a hug that went just beyond concerned excitement to slightly painful.

"Let go of me, Mother," Taylor said quietly. Tourists were pulling out their cameras and flashes started to blind her. Her mother's thin hands tightened on her shoulders, causing her to wince.

"This man is trying to kill you. We're here to take you home and protect you."

Trey pushed his chair back and slowly rose to his full height. He towered over her parents, even when he leaned over and placed both hands flat on the table. "Right now, you're the only ones hurting your daughter. You're also about to cause a scene. Let go of her and walk out while you can."

"You can't touch me here. I'll have you arrested so fast you won't have time to blink," her mother hissed.

"He can't, but I sure as hell can," Casey said forcefully as she stopped next to Taylor with a shotgun resting comfortably in her hands. "Now get out of my diner."

Taylor felt the painful hold of her mother's hand release as she looked around. The tourists may have been snapping their cameras at first, but now they sat side by side with the locals, wearing the same fierce expressions on their faces. They weren't going to mock her; they were going to stand with her.

"Mother, I've had enough," Taylor said with a

confidence she didn't know she had. "I'm filing a harassment report with the sheriff tomorrow. And don't ever touch me again."

Her parents glanced around and saw the tide had turned against them. With a quick tightening of her jaw, her mother spun on her heel and walked out of the diner with her father trailing after.

"Something changed in you," Trey said quietly as the diners went back to eating.

"When the cameras came out, I didn't panic. And when my mother's hand tightened, I didn't panic. Somehow I felt strong enough to handle it all and I plan to do just that. When Sheriff Wilson gives me an update tomorrow, I'll tell him about my parents. There's no need to be embarrassed about them anymore. I need to treat them as the threat they are. But for now, I want to get home and curl up on the couch with you and a bottle of wine."

Trey smiled at her as he paid the bill. "That sounds perfect."

Taylor wrapped her hand through the crook of his elbow and let him lead her home.

Chapter Nine

Trey and Taylor unlocked their door and froze. A beeping noise filled the living room. Looking around, Trey caught sight of his laptop sitting open. The beeping started again and Taylor looked around the room.

"It's my computer. Someone is calling me."

"Probably Morris wanting to gossip," Taylor joked.

"I'm telling you, men don't gossip," Trey turned the laptop around and answered the call.

"Worse than the Rose . . ." Taylor started before being cut off.

"Hello? Are they there? Why can't I see anything?"

"I don't know, Lily Rae. If you'd move your big head, then I could see."

"Don't tell me what to do, Daisy Mae. It's not like you're fifty anymore. You don't know about this anymore than I do."

"Wait, what does this button do?" Suddenly the screen came alive and three white heads came into view. "Oh, I fixed it!"

"Good job, Violet Fae." Miss Lily praised before leaning very close to the camera. "Can you see us, dears?"

Trey tried not to laugh. "Yes, Miss Lily, we can see you."

"Oh, excellent. We heard our dear girl has had a rough

day and we wanted to see how you're doing," Miss Lily said as the three white heads bobbed in and out of the camera.

"Doing better now that I see you three," Taylor said with tears filling her eyes. This was family, not the woman clawing at her for money.

"Oh don't cry, dear. We'll take care of you," Miss Violet cooed as she leaned forward filling the computer screen with her puffy bosom. A tear ran down Taylor's cheek. It really was just like being at home.

"When we heard about your day, we got you something," Miss Daisy said as she pushed her sisters out of the way of the camera. A knock at the door had Trey and Taylor looking at each other in confusion. "Ah, right on time. You two enjoy it and know we're here for you if you need us."

"That's right!" Miss Lily and Miss Violet said as they battled for camera time.

"Okay, turn it off."

"How do you turn it off?"

"Can't you just hang it up?"

"How do you hang up a computer?"

"Maybe if we click . . ." The screen went blank and Taylor found herself crying for a completely different reason. She and Trey were laughing so hard they forgot about the knock at the door until it sounded again.

Trey shook his head in wonder and opened the door. "Nabi! What are you doing here?"

"I come bearing gifts from the Rose sisters." Nabi held out a huge basket and set it on the coffee table.

Taylor gave him a quick hug and then opened the basket. She pulled out a pitcher of Rose Sister tea minus the ice, a container of chicken salad, and a chocolate chip pecan pie. "You flew all the way here just to give this to us? Thank you so much."

"The pleasure is mine. The kids have decided to wage war on the security personnel. Zain and Gabe have decided they want to be spies and are constantly trying to take us out with water balloons while they lay siege to the cottage. Their goal being to overrun and take control of the cottage where we control all the farm's security. They told Abigail she couldn't play with them because girls couldn't be spies. Trouble is, little four-and-a-half-year-old Abby is much sneakier than both boys. She actually got into the cottage today and locked down the whole farm until Ahmed and Mo were able to break into the cottage. Abby was twirling on the chair and looked up at the two men and said, 'Mommy was right. I am better than the boys.'"

Taylor laughed. She laughed so hard tears threatened again. Abby was beautiful with Ahmed's tan skin, Bridget's blue eyes, and the cutest little braid for her hair. "Oh, she's going to be so much trouble."

"Going to be? She already is. Dani was so furious at the boys for starting this that I thought it would be a good time to offer my assistance to the Roses while the kids get their punishment tonight."

"How did the Rose sisters even find out? I guess it was on the news," Taylor wondered.

"John found out an hour before it hit the news. The ladies were upset to say the least, but they feel they won the battle since they sent food."

Taylor pulled out a knife and brought some plates and glasses into the room. She cut up the pie and poured everyone a glass of special tea. "Well, we appreciate this more than we can say. I'm just sorry we had to take you away from a young lady, perhaps?"

"Smooth, sweetheart," Trey whispered as he tried not to laugh.

Nabi didn't bother to look embarrassed. He was single and lived in Keeneston. He would be asked about it everyday. Heck, there were active bets being placed on it at the café already.

"No one yet. But, I am only thirty. There is plenty of time for me to settle down. Besides, I don't have much time to date. I'm, how do you say it . . . married to my work. Speaking of which, I must be going. I am flying to Rahmi to pick up Princess Ameera and her son. They are visiting Keeneston for a couple weeks."

Trey and Taylor stood along with Nabi and walked him to the door. "We can't thank you enough. We'll see you in Keeneston soon. I don't think I can stay away until Thanksgiving."

"As always, it will be a pleasure." Nabi walked down the path and slid into his car.

"Let's see what else is in there," Taylor said excitedly as she rushed back to the basket.

Trey sat down next to Taylor on the couch as they pulled out some issues of the *Keeneston Journal* from Gemma, a stun gun from Cy, crayon drawings from Riley and Reagan, and a binder full of new plays and workout routines from Cade and Will.

Curling up in Trey's arms, Taylor took a sip of Rose Sister ice tea and read the gossip while Trey flipped through the new plays. It was the perfect end to a horrible day. All thanks to their adopted family.

Trey wiped his sweaty palms on his jeans as he and Taylor

moved forward in line. Finally, everything was perfect. Taylor was eating cotton candy, he'd won a pink unicorn for her, and the lights from the carnival were casting a warm glow on them as they stepped up to the Ferris wheel.

Taylor laid her head against his shoulder and took a pinch of her cotton candy before they stepped closer to the ride. Trey handed over their tickets and reached his hand into his pocket as they took a seat. The bar was locked in place and the time was finally right.

"Isn't that the weirdest thing?" Taylor said with a bit of a shiver.

"What?" Trey asked as they rose into the night sky.

"That clown."

"What clown?"

"The one with the rainbow hair and big red nose," Taylor pointed over the side of the Ferris wheel and Trey looked over.

Sure enough there stood a clown with big oversized hands on hips and one big red shoe tapping the ground as it stared up at them. "It's watching us."

"I know. It's giving me the creeps. I hate clowns."

"I've never minded them, but this one is bothering me. Why won't he look away?"

Taylor looked down at the clown and locked eyes with it. "It won't stop staring," she said in wonder.

Trey slipped his hand over the ring, but the damn clown wouldn't look away. There was no way he was proposing when Taylor was creeped out by this clown tapping his foot and staring at them. Then to hammer the last nail into the proposal coffin, Taylor's phone started beeping.

"Oh! The set has been cleared and we're filming in an hour. I'm sorry. Tonight has been so much fun, but we've already fallen behind in filming."

"It's okay. I understand." Trey pushed the ring back in his pocket and put his arm around Taylor for the last part of the ride. The clown was nowhere to be seen when they got off the Ferris wheel.

Trey drove Taylor home in silence. His mind was thinking of the past. Taylor had come to every single one of his games—even when she was in the middle of studying. She'd hide out in the crowd, wearing jeans and a sweatshirt, and cheer for him. And now, when she deserved to be in the spotlight, he can't seem to find the moment. He was a failure at proposing.

Taylor smiled at the cameras as she left the resort. Grant was still in front of the tired reporters giving them a reenactment of his heroics from the other night. She was exhausted. Filming had gone well and Melanie had finally done what she was told. But that had only come when she saw Cyndi Lu in the bushes. Thinking it was a photographer, Melanie amped up her acting skills.

"Taylor? Are you okay?" The soft words spooked her and she spun around so fast she almost lost her balance. Cyndi Lu stood behind a trashcan, one large red shoe poking out the side.

"Yes. But you have to stop scaring me, Cyndi. Popping up like this," Taylor looked pointedly at her shoes, "Following me to the carnival with Trey. You're a great fan, and I appreciate the support, but . . ."

Cyndi Lu sighed. "But you don't want me around either."

"I didn't say that. I just ask that you pick your moments

better. You're a sweet girl, but you should be in college somewhere driving the boys crazy and hanging out with your friends. Not following me around. As you've noticed, I'm kinda boring," Taylor smiled kindly.

"Okay. I'll give you space. But he doesn't deserve you. No one does, including me." Cyndi Lu hung her head and disappeared into the shadows.

Taylor's shoulders slumped. She was such a sweet girl who had so much more potential than following her around and diving in dumpsters. Taylor got in her car and was thankful it was just a couple minutes to her house. She turned on the music and opened the windows as she pulled onto Hangman's Highway.

The salt air washed over her face as Taylor sang a Maroon 5 song playing on the radio. The moon was almost full and reflected off the ocean so brightly she almost missed the headlights filling her rearview mirror.

Taylor stopped singing when the car behind blinded her. She tried to wave them around, but the large truck just ignored her and closed in even more. Fighting the urge to speed up, Taylor started to slow down as she entered a curve on the road. The truck's large engine revved and the horrific sound of metal and fiberglass crunching was the only thing she heard before being shot off the road.

Taylor screamed, her hands reflexively coming up to protect her face as her car left the road and flew over the embankment. With a jarring impact that caused the airbags to deploy, Taylor slammed head first into darkness.

Blinking her eyes, Taylor came to. She didn't know how long she had been out, but it couldn't have been long. Maroon 5 was still singing on her radio. It was then she felt the water. She had come to a stop in the ocean. Waves were lapping at the car as the tide tried to pull her further into the ocean.

Taylor felt panic clawing at her, but knew she didn't have time for it. She shoved at the airbag and unbuckled her seatbelt. Taylor grabbed her things from the car before climbing out the open window. The water was only at her calves and treasure hunters were running toward her. She was safe for now.

Chapter Ten

Trey was dreaming of fighting a clown when the phone woke him up. He reached out and answered without opening his eyes. Taylor's scared voice had him shooting out of bed and running out the door before he realized he was naked.

"I'll be right there, honey. Are the police there? Are you safe?" Trey asked as he rushed back inside and stepped into some athletic clothes.

"I'm fine. Just scared. Hurry, Trey."

In all his years by her side and on the football field, Trey had never felt so useless as he did now. He wasn't there and she needed him.

"I'm just minutes away, sweetheart. I'm coming, I'm coming," Trey spoke as calmly as he could as he started the car and peeled out of the driveway.

His heart pounded as he sped down the highway. He saw the flashing lights reflecting off the ocean first. Then he saw the tow truck as it hauled Taylor's car from the ocean. He frantically slammed on his brakes and searched wildly for her. It was only when he'd raced onto the beach that he saw her looking so small in the back of the ambulance with an icepack on her face.

"Taylor!" Trey had her wrapped in his arms protecting her from the flashing cameras before he even knew it.

"I'm okay. Just bruised," she mumbled against his chest.

Trey leaned back and looked down at her face. A bruise was forming around her eye from the airbag and one was starting to form on her sternum from her seatbelt. "I don't know what I'd do if something happened to you. Taylor, I love you. My life just isn't worth it without you in it."

Trey clutched Taylor to her chest as he held on to her for dear life.

She watched from behind the news van as pain contorted Trey's face. He held Taylor so close to him. She got the feeling he would fight dragons to protect her. At that moment she believed he would. And Taylor. She didn't look like a woman settling. She looked like a woman completely in love. The way Taylor clung to Trey and looked at him–she didn't like to admit it, but she'd been wrong. She had thought to separate them. She thought he didn't deserve her. But in this moment, she realized she was wrong.

Cyndi Lu put one big red shoe in front of the other and left the beach.

Trey refused to let Taylor walk. He carried her from the car and into the house. They hadn't said much over the past hour. Instead they just kept constant contact with each other. The only way he knew she was safe was to feel her in his arms.

"I can't believe there are no leads. Do you think it was your stalker? You should have told the sheriff's deputy about her."

"Tell Junior? If you didn't notice, he was too busy checking out my legs to pay attention."

"He was?"

"He's a sweet guy, but a bit of a horn dog. And there isn't anything to tell him. Cyndi Lu is harmless. She would never hurt me."

"I find it so strange that you're on a first-name basis with your stalker." Trey shook his head in disbelief. "But if you don't think it's her, then who would do this?" Trey asked as she set her down on the couch.

He walked into the kitchen to pour her a glass of Rose Sister ice tea and then hurried back to her side. "Here, this will make you feel better."

"This will make me so drunk I won't feel anything . . . which is just perfect." Taylor took a drink and leaned back against him and shivered. "Do you think it could be my parents? I mentioned them to Junior. If I married, then they would have no right to any of my money. You would. Do you think this is because I'm not letting them back in my life? They may think it's easier to kill me and claim my estate than to get me to work with them again."

"I know your parents hurt you, but do you really think they'd kill you?"

"Sadly, I don't know. I hope not. I've always held out some small chance that they'd come back into my life as good people, but I think I can get rid of that fantasy. Mom was high on something last time I saw her," she said, frustrated.

"Whoever it is won't get to you so easily again. You need security."

"If you hand me the phone, then I'll give my old crew a call and see if they can fly out to help me." Trey reached for her purse and dug around it until he felt her phone.

Taylor dialed her old security firm in Los Angeles. The emergency operator picked up and patched her through to the owner in less than five minutes. Taylor told him what was happening on Hung Island and asked if he had a full protection team available. She hated it—the feeling of being constantly surrounded. But even tonight was enough to freak her out.

"I'm sorry, Miss Jefferies. I can't get a team out there, but I know someone in Georgia who would be perfect for you. I'll call them and they will have a team sent to you by the morning."

"Are they good?" Taylor asked. She was wary of having people around her she didn't know.

"The best. I'd use them."

Taylor hung up the phone and smiled softly at Trey. "A team will be here tomorrow. There's someone in Georgia they're contracting to protect me."

"Are they any good? I want the best and only the best."

"Supposedly they are. They'll be here in the morning so you can feel secure in going to practice."

"Go to practice? How can I . . ."

"Trey, it's why we got the security. They'll be with me and you can focus on your job. I need to focus on mine without you hovering," Taylor said as she reached up and cupped his cheek with her hand.

She could tell Trey wasn't happy about it, but he realized it was a losing argument. "Fine, but I'm going to tuck you into bed." Trey scooped her up and carried her into the back of the house as she laughed.

"Thank you. That short hallway was so dangerous, my handsome knight." Taylor kissed his cheek and after being put down she walked into the bathroom to take out her contacts. Knowing she was safe and knowing she had a man who loved her made her feel so much better.

What didn't make her feel better was the pounding headache or her aching chest. Trey had her in a death grip as he slept. Taylor managed to pry herself out and get some medicine. She opened the door and stepped out into the night air. It always calmed her and helped chase the headache away.

She looked up to the full moon and out at the sparkling ocean as she walked into the coffee table on their porch. So, she'd walked out without her glasses. Oh well, she could still enjoy the warm breeze regardless if everything was fuzzy around her.

Taylor saw the vague outline of the porch swing and sat slowly down on it. She closed her eyes and took a deep, calming breath. The rhythmic crashing of the waves calmed her headache as she finally felt her body start to relax. It didn't last long, though. Clicking noises and then a low rumble had her eyes shooting open. Taylor squinted and then saw the source of the noise.

"Oh, aren't you a cute puppy?" Taylor cooed as she held out her hand for the dog to sniff. The large dog's tail started to thump on the wood porch as he nuzzled her hand. Taylor stroked his massive head and scratched behind his ears.

The dog shoved his head between her legs and tried to goose her. "Whoa. That's not for you," Taylor laughed as she pushed the dog back. His big pink tongue licked her hand happily as his tail continued to wag.

Then with a quick hook of his paw, the overly excited dog grabbed a hold of her leg and starting humping.

"No! Bad dog!" Taylor tried to push the dog off, but his green eyes just glowed happily as his tongue hung out.

Finally with a big push, she dislodged the dog. "Where are your manners?"

The dog gave a little whine in response and then rolled onto his back at her feet. "Much better." Taylor leaned over and scratched his tummy as she thought about what would happen tomorrow.

Tomorrow her old life would come back. Her parents, the bodyguards, the cameras — she just hoped she could handle it all. Taylor drifted to sleep on the porch with the dog at her feet. Maybe she should get a dog. Discounting the crotch sniffing and humping, she felt safe with the big hairy boy. But as the sun began to rise, the dog got up and loped away. It was time to go back inside and prepare to face her fears.

Chapter Eleven

Trey couldn't stop watching Taylor as she got ready for the day. It was secretly one of his favorite things about being a couple. The ritual of her washing her face and putting on moisturizer, down to the way she shimmied into her jeans. It was a show all for him, and only him. Such intimate details that only he was privileged to. For some reason, it made him inordinately proud.

The ringing of the doorbell halted his viewing pleasure as Taylor reached behind to fasten her bra. "That's my new security team. Could you get it?" she called from the bathroom.

"Sure." Trey finished tying his shoe and headed to answer the door.

He unlocked the deadbolt and pulled the door open wide. He felt his brow come together in confusion as he looked at the blonde knockout in stilettos standing at the door. She and Taylor could be twins except for the fact she looked to be a couple years older, probably in her early thirties. She had to be an actress though.

"Can I help you?"

"Hi, Trey." The blonde reached out and Trey automatically shook her hand. "I'm Taylor's security."

"Oh, great. Where's the rest of your team?"

The woman just smiled. "I'm all that's available, but

don't worry; I won't get taken down three yards from the end zone like you did against New York." The woman walked past him and into the living room as Taylor hurried from the bedroom.

"Are you from the security company? Where's the team?" Taylor asked as she stopped next to Trey.

"I am your team. I'm Mallory Westin of Westin Security. I figured if you were anything like me, then you didn't want a bunch of hulking men surrounding you. Personally, it always made me feel claustrophobic."

Taylor nodded. "Exactly. It's so nice to meet you." Taylor and Mallory shook hands before Mallory started to look around.

"Where would you like me to put my bag?"

"Oh. I thought they had told you. I don't need live-in security. I just need someone while I'm working and for transportation. If you could drop me off at home each night and pick me up in the morning according to my movie schedule, then I think we'll be good. That and tell me where you got those shoes," Taylor laughed.

"I don't recommend it, but it's your call. When I did research on the island, I saw a vacation house to rent just a half-mile away. I can stay there. Let me have a look at your security system and make sure it's up to par, though."

"Great. You can do that while I finish getting ready. Then it's off to the set in about twenty minutes." Taylor smiled as Mallory nodded and headed back into the bedroom.

Trey watched as Mallory examined the system and started making alterations. "Do you really think you can keep her safe?"

"Do you really think you can rush for more than fifty yards against Florida this season?"

Trey grinned. "Touché."

✫ ✫ ✫

Trey grunted and pushed with all he had over and over again as sweat dripped down his face. The weights on the bench press clanked down when the set was done. Morris sauntered over and looked in disgust at the two hundred and twenty-five pounds on the bar.

"Twenty-two reps? You running backs are wimps."

"At least I'm not the quarterback. They don't even have to lift heavy weights," Trey teased Tucker.

Morris laughed as he laid down on the bench press. "Bet I can do thirty-five reps and put y'all to shame."

"What are we betting?" Trey asked as he wiped his face with a towel.

"How about a date with that hot bodyguard? I mean, damn. I looked her up after you told us about her and she is smokin'," Morris said as Christian and Tucker nodded.

"Somehow I don't think she'd let me pass her off as a bet," Trey said as he moved to spot Morris.

"A man can dream. Speaking of dreaming, are you paying attention here? I'm at twenty-four and still talking," Morris goaded them.

The men rolled their eyes as Morris put them to shame on the bench press. "Hello? Earth to Everett," Christian waved his hand in front of Trey's face.

"Huh? Oh sorry. I'm trying to think of a way to propose to Taylor. Everything I've tried has been ruined. The carnival would have been perfect if not for that freaking clown."

"Why don't you just grow a pair and ask her?" Tucker asked.

"It's not that easy. She deserves more than that."

"That may be, but did you hear about Richardson's

wife?" Christian said in a low whisper.

"No, what?" Trey asked as they gathered closer to hear the latest news.

Taylor looked at the watch Mallory handed her and slid it onto her wrist. "So, if I press here it'll send you my location?" Taylor asked.

"That's right. I'll know it's an emergency and will be there in a flash. Now, how do you want to play this? I can be the big bad bodyguard or the pushy assistant."

Taylor looked out at the sea of media. Grant somehow lost his shirt and glistened as he made his way on to the set. Melanie had three hulking bodyguards surrounding her with earpieces and matching tight black t-shirts. "I don't think they'd believe me if I said you were a bodyguard. Your clothes are too nice."

Mallory laughed and it somehow eased Taylor's nerves. "Oh, I can pull off mean bodyguard with the best of them. However, I didn't think it was your style."

"It's not. Let's just get me through press row as fast as possible."

"Okay, let's go. And don't worry about a thing. I'll take care of all questions, pushy press, and divas."

Taylor opened the door with a slight smile playing at her lips. She really liked Mallory and her stress level was already falling as Mallory kept up a steady stream of light conversation.

Press row wasn't nearly as bad as she thought it was going to be. Taylor talked to Millie, and when it appeared the other stations were getting pushy, Mallory simply stepped in and announced they were late for a meeting with Jim and hurried her onto set.

"You're either brave or stupid," Melanie said from her make-up chair.

"Excuse me?" Taylor tried to keep the bite from her voice, but failed. It didn't appear Melanie noticed, though.

"I thought after your trailer incident you'd get some security. Instead you broke the cardinal rule—you hired an assistant hotter than you."

"I don't think that's possible, but it's pretty darn close. You two are like a wet dream come true," Grant grinned as bronzer was applied to his abs.

Taylor saw Mallory roll her eyes and decided to let it go.

Unfortunately, Melanie wasn't going to let anything go. "See, the more important you are, the more security you should have. As I'm the most important person on set, I have my men here looking out for me. I guess it just goes to show you're not important as you think."

"Melanie, dear." Taylor took her time putting her fake smile on. "I'm sorry to tell you, you broke your own rule and hired more attractive people than yourself, too. Poor thing, you didn't even realize it." Taylor spun on her heel as Melanie took her time registering the insult. "And if you don't hit your marks today, I'll be forced to cut some of your scenes and focus on Grant's character more."

Taylor walked out with Mallory trailing behind her. Curse words floated around as Melanie spat them as fast as she could.

"Cut!" Jim yelled and the boom mics dropped on the set. "I think we got it. I'll review it tonight and let you know. Good job, everyone."

Taylor jotted down some notes before reaching for her

bag. After a full day of working with Mallory, they were already used to each other's movements. Mallory had Taylor's bag in hand and handed it to her along with her phone.

"Trey called you and then me. I gave him an update about thirty minutes ago."

"Thanks. Wow, are you sure I can't hire you full time? You actually make me like security." Taylor said goodbye to the crew and dialed Trey as she followed Mallory out of Seawave Resort.

"Hey, sweetheart. How is Mallory doing?" Trey asked once he picked up.

"Great. It's been smooth sailing all day. Do we need to pick up dinner on the way home?" Taylor asked as Mallory opened the door to her SUV for Taylor.

"Well, that's why I was calling. The guys and I got to talking and they invited me out to dinner. I didn't want to commit before talking to you."

"That's fine. Are you doing your night run as well? You know it's treasure night, so it may be crowded."

"I know, but it helps me think so I'll probably go for my run after dinner and then head home before you go to bed."

"Just don't fall in a pit the treasure hunters will all be digging. And if you find the treasure, I get half," Taylor laughed before saying goodbye.

"Treasure?" Mallory asked. "Trey is on the hunt for the Hung Island treasure? I can't believe it."

Taylor shook her head. "Oh no. He's not a treasure hunter. Every third night, he goes for a long run on the beach. He missed it the other night and he was just telling me he's going now. He's out to dinner with the guys right now, which gives me an idea. Girls' night at the diner."

"Sounds good."

Mallory drove to Casey's and was surprised to get a table after only a couple minutes. They both ordered burgers, fries, and milkshakes as talk of the treasure hunt filled the diner.

"This place is great," Mallory said as she finished the last bite of her burger.

"I know. This was so much fun." Taylor paused and looked guiltily at Mallory. "Can I ask you a personal question?"

"Sure."

"Do you have a boyfriend at home? If so, how do you make it work?"

"Actually I don't. I was dating someone in the Secret Service, but it just didn't work out. I can't believe you and Trey would be having problems."

"No, we're not. Well, not really. We've been together for seven years and it never bothered me before. But after going through all this, I find myself wondering why suddenly being boyfriend and girlfriend isn't enough. I mean, we know we're meant for each other."

"But he's dragging his feet?" When Taylor nodded, Mallory just grinned. "When has a man ever done the right thing? I think it's pretty clear he loves you. My best friend, Elle, just got engaged. So I understand that nagging feeling of needing to do the same, but with you it's different from me. See, while I was asked a million times about a special someone, the truth is there hasn't been anyone in a long time. But you have someone. Someone who I bet is anxiously waiting for you to give him a clear signal that you're ready for the next step. 'Cause we both know it takes a flashing neon sign for guys to get the hint."

Taylor took a sip of her milkshake and thought about it. "You know, I think you're right. I just need to tell Trey I'm ready for more. I bet he's just waiting for me to figure out that I was ready." Taylor paused and looked Mallory over. She was so put-together, but there was something sad about the way she looked. "Did you have *it* once?"

"I thought I did," Mallory shrugged. Her phone beeped, interrupting any follow-up questions Taylor was going to ask. "This is my friend's sister. She's having trouble with some architect or something. If you're ready to go home, then I'll get you all locked up and safe for Trey. Then I need to do some research at the rental."

"Yeah, I'm ready. Lock me up, jailer," Taylor teased as they headed home.

Chapter Twelve

Trey pulled over at the end of the bridge and parked his car at the marina and locked it. The full moon and the energy surrounding the treasure hunt had him longing to hit the sand. It would also give him the time he needed to think of the perfect proposal for Taylor. The carnival was a bust. Maybe he could try dinner again. And the guys had suggested using the stadium for a picnic on the fifty-yard line.

He put his headphones on and let his mind go blank. He took off down the familiar path toward the beach. If he pushed it, he'd be able to run almost to the resort and then home. Taylor and Mallory could take him to get his car in the morning.

Taylor licked the ice cream from her spoon as she sat by the large bay window and watched the treasure hunters digging up the beach. Some were standing on ladders ordering others to dig, some were walking around with metal detectors, and others were dancing around a bonfire trying to conduct a séance so the pirate captain himself could tell them the location of the treasure.

She may not admit it, but Taylor loved the treasure

hunt. Not necessarily the actually hunting part, but the way the town seemed to hum with energy and optimism. It was contagious. Her phone interrupted the chanting of the séance. Taylor clicked the new email and groaned. They were being called in for a reshoot in thirty minutes. She checked her watch and nibbled on her lower lip. Mallory was working on something, and this was an unscheduled shoot. She should be safe. After all, if something happened, she had her watch and could send an emergency signal to Mallory.

Grabbing a piece of paper from the kitchen, Taylor left a note for Trey and grabbed her scripts and notes. Taylor was sure Melanie's mistakes were the reason for the reshoot. It was so frustrating. When Melanie was on, she was breathtaking. However, getting her to act like that was worse than pulling nails.

Taylor parked next to the back entrance of the ballroom where they'd been filming that day. She used her key and hurried inside. She wanted to beat everyone there so she could have a word with Jim to see what they could do to get Melanie acting better, literally and figuratively.

The ballroom lights were off and she fumbled for a minute until she found the switch. The lights cast a low glow as they warmed up and the shadows seemed to move. Taylor felt the hair on her arms stand up and suddenly realized this had not been a good idea. Oh crap, she'd just pulled a bimbo move.

"Hello?" she called out.

"Oh thank goodness! It's spooky in here," Melanie laughed as she walked in from another entrance. Taylor let out a nervous laugh. She'd totally been jumping at shadows. "I guess we're the only ones who read the messages from the tech line."

"Grant's probably too busy looking at himself in the mirror to check his email. Do you know which scene we're filming?" Taylor asked as she walked toward Melanie.

The door Taylor had just come through opened an inch and then slammed shut behind her. Taylor and Melanie jumped and stared at it as they held their breaths. Taylor found her watch by touch and pressed the panic button.

Trey wound the way past his house and smiled to himself as he saw the light on in the kitchen. Taylor was probably raiding the ice cream he'd picked up for her. She loved ice cream . . . maybe he should put the ring in it? No, she could eat it and that wouldn't be romantic. Trey's smile fell from his face. He'd run several miles now and still hadn't come up with a perfect proposal. At this rate, he'd never get married.

Trey was so lost in thought he almost didn't see the woman running toward him with her arms flailing and pigtails flapping. His eyes went wide and he tried to run around her but Cyndi Lu leapt at him. Trey tried to jump out of the way, but Cyndi Lu wrapped her arms around his leg. As he ran, he dragged her along the sand as if she were a toddler in full tantrum.

"Get off of me!" Trey yelled as he pulled his ear buds out. He lifted his leg and shook it, but Cyndi Lu held strong.

"No! You have to listen to me," Cyndi Lu wailed.

"Dammit," Trey grunted as he jumped on one leg trying to dislodge Cyndi Lu.

"It's Taylor. I think she's in danger," Cyndi called from

the ground as she clung to his leg.

"Yeah, in danger from you," Trey shot out as he changed tactics and started dragging Cyndi Lu down the beach to look for a cop. He was nearing the resort and there would be one around somewhere.

"No. I would never hurt Taylor. She's so kind to me."

Trey stopped and looked down at her still latched around his ankle. "Fine. I'm listening. Why is she in danger?"

"She went back to the set tonight and they're not scheduled to film."

"So? Mallory's with her and they have reshoots all the time."

"But Mallory wasn't with her and no one else was there either. When I peeked in the door, the only person there was Melanie. Melanie hates Taylor. I mean, hate, hate, hates her. Please, just go check it out."

Trey thought back to all the trouble Melanie had caused. It was true; she gave Taylor a hard time on set. But could she really be the danger? "Okay. Let's go check it out. Let me call a cab."

"No need. My car is right there." Cyndi Lu started running up the beach to the public parking lot just as Mallory's SUV went flying by. Oh shit, something was terribly wrong.

Trey looked at the tiny yellow electric car. "I don't think I'm going to fit."

"I'll open the sunroof. Come on!" Cyndi's pigtails fluttered behind her as she ran to her car.

Taylor finally let go of the breath she was holding. No one was there and now she felt kind of silly. At least Melanie was here with her. She'd give Jim another ten minutes and then call to see what was going on. It was obvious he hadn't filled Melanie in on it either.

"How do you think filming is going so far?" Melanie asked as she walked around the equipment set up from that afternoon's shoot.

Taylor shrugged as she thought of a polite way to respond. In full honesty, Melanie was dying a slow and horrendous death on film. "Well, I saw the footage from the beach scene and it's good," Taylor said diplomatically. Good was about the nicest thing she could say about it. Grant, as much as she hated to give him credit, was fabulous. Melanie, not so much. She was so fake that it came off as corny. She and Jim were still unsure how to proceed.

"Good? I was spectacular. If this film weren't a stupid romantic comedy, I'd earn an Oscar!" Melanie spat, suddenly furious. She jumped up from the actor's chair and started pacing in front of where Taylor sat.

"Well . . ." Taylor started hesitantly.

"But no. I get stuck on this piece-of-crap movie with a narcissistic lead actor, an asshole director, and a producer who is too young and stupid to know what she's doing."

"Excuse me?" Taylor stood up slowly and narrowed her eyes. "I may be young, but I've been in this business for more years than you. I know it inside and out. What I don't know, I do everything in my power to learn. That's more than you can say. Your whining, pouting, and constant refusal to listen have put us almost a week behind schedule and we just started principal filming."

"My whining has been solely about you. You get in the

way constantly. You're nothing but a baby that has spun a spell on Hollywood so they let you pretend to produce. I need my moments in the spotlight, but you have some personal vendetta against me."

Taylor stopped what she was about to say. "What are you talking about? I don't have a vendetta against you. I was the one that pushed for you to have this part."

"Really? Then why, tell me, are you constantly in front of the media? You're chatting up the reporters like a politician. I'm the one who needs that. If I don't get the attention I deserve, then I may not get another part—even a crappy part like this one. I'm thirty-one years old and a year older than Grant. I've almost aged out of Hollywood. Another couple years are all I have left before I'm cast only as a middle-aged mom. But then you decide to come back and steal the limelight . . . *my* limelight. You're all Hollywood is talking about, not me!" Melanie screamed as she grabbed the metal boom mic stand and swung.

Taylor was so surprised she almost didn't move. But somewhere in the primal part of her brain, it registered she was under attack. She dropped to the ground and the boom mic cut through the air above her. Taylor crawled on hands and knees behind the chair. But Melanie was advancing on her again. The mic crashed down on the chair, knocking it to the ground and breaking its wooden leg.

Taylor grabbed the leg and blocked the next shot from the boom mic.

"I hate you! You've ruined my life!" Melanie screeched as she swung the mic stand again.

"And you think killing me is going to help you?" Taylor gasped as she darted behind a big trunk of props.

"Oh yes. I'll be front and center at the funeral and dedicate my performance to you. I'll make the media rounds talking about how wonderful you were and how blessed I was to work with you, even if our time was cut short. I'll tell them all about how you thought I was the best actress out there and how it was your dream for us to win an Oscar. We'll be nominated for sure."

"It was you." Taylor was so shocked she almost got a mic to the head. "You're the one who set the fire and who pushed me off the road."

"Of course it was! That stupid groundskeeper didn't even see me as I walked by and tipped the gas can. And the police had no idea it was me who ran you off the road. My performance was so compelling that they never even interviewed me," Melanie laughed.

But then the laughter stopped and Melanie lunged over the trunk. Taylor didn't have time to think. She brought the wooden chair leg down as hard as she could. The back door to the ballroom was ripped open right as the chair leg splintered over Melanie's head. Trey, Cyndi Lu, and Mallory raced in.

Taylor let out a relieved breath as she shakily turned to them. Trey's eyes went wide only a split second before he sprinted toward Taylor. Cyndi Lu let out a war cry and Mallory hurtled production equipment in four-inch heels.

"What?" was all Taylor got out before Trey's shoulder collided with her midsection. The air was pushed out of her lungs as they crashed on to the floor. Her eyes went wide in horror as she watched the boom mic slam against Trey's back.

"Get off of her!" Melanie yelled at Trey as she raised the boom mic stand again.

Suddenly Melanie wasn't there. In a flash of blonde hair and pearls, Melanie and Mallory went flying over the trunk and landed on the other side. Taylor blinked as a blur of pigtails leapt onto the trunk above her. With a cry of anger, Cyndi Lu did a driving elbow drop, the likes she'd only seen in professional wrestling, off the trunk and disappeared from sight. Melanie's screaming died suddenly and was replaced with gasping sounds.

Trey looked on in complete disbelief at Taylor before anger and fear filled his eyes. "What the hell were you thinking coming here alone?"

"I'm sorry. It was so stupid of me. I thought the person after me wouldn't know about the change of schedule and I left you a note for you to come pick me up. I thought a five-minute drive here was all I had to worry about."

Trey leaned down and kissed her hard. He had almost lost her to a crazy diva. He wasn't ever letting go of her. As if a vision from above, he knew what he had to do.

Standing up and stretching out his throbbing back, he helped Taylor up. They both stepped forward and looked over the trunk. One perfect stiletto was pressed against Melanie's throat while the skewed pigtailed stalker sat on her.

"How do you run in those heels?" Cyndi asked reverently.

Mallory shrugged one perfect shoulder without a single hair out of place. "It's a talent. Just like knowing all the stats of the Vultures and making the perfect pitcher of sweet tea."

"I think you just lost your stalker," Trey whispered to her.

Taylor laughed and wrapped her arm around his as Junior and some of the other deputies rushed into the room with weapons drawn.

"I think I lost my favorite horny deputy, too," Taylor teased as they watched Junior strut around Mallory, his eyes shining with excitement.

"You know what you haven't lost?" Trey asked as he wrapped his arms around her waist.

"Hmm?"

"Me." Trey kissed her gently then. She was his life and there was no more waiting. Tomorrow would be the beginning of their new life together, come hell or high water. And he just happened to know someone even the devil wouldn't cross who could make it happen.

Chapter Thirteen

The clock lights glowed blue in the dark bedroom as Trey stared up at the ceiling. When they had gotten home, he'd made love to her over and over again, just thankful to have her in his arms. Her adrenaline had worn off and she was now sound asleep next to him. But his was still pumping through his body.

Turning on his side, he stared at his cell phone sitting next to the bed. It was four o'clock in the morning. He knew what he had to do. Sliding naked from the tangled sheets, he grabbed his phone and slipped on a pair of athletic shorts before sneaking out the front of the house.

He dialed a number he knew by heart and waited for the sleepy voice to answer.

"I need help," Trey said when the phone was picked up.

The lights blinded her, the camera clicks were deafening, and panic threatened to strangle her throat. Mallory held up one perfectly manicured hand and smiled with such cold precision that Taylor shivered. And so did the media. They took a collective step away from Taylor as Trey placed a protective arm around her and led her into the ballroom where the actors and production crew were gathered.

"It's strange being back here. It looks so innocent and just last night it was nearly the place of my death," Taylor whispered to Trey.

He squeezed her shoulder in silent support and Taylor took a deep breath to try to relax. She was safe, she kept repeating over and over again. She didn't know if she could do this today. Looking around at the dejected faces of the crew, she knew she'd done the right thing.

Jim cleared his throat and stood up. "This was a hard lot to have thrown on you and while we all believe in this project, we understand putting it on indefinite hold."

The crew nodded, the disappointment clear on their faces. Sure they cared for her, but some of the people she'd hired were veterans on their way out of the industry. Others were newbies just thankful for a chance and Melanie had ruined that for them.

Taylor stepped away from Trey and folded her hands in front of her. "Thank you all for being so supportive and understanding. We've lost our lead actress. This shoot has had more incidents than I care to remember. It seems that fate was against us . . ."

The crew nodded and dropped their heads. Some kicked their feet quietly against the carpet as they waited to be laid off.

"Just as it seemed fate was against Darin and Kathy. But he found her against all odds. He didn't give up and, with an order of roses, started a courtship that lasted their whole lives. And I'm not going to give up, either."

Heads shot up and feet stopped kicking imaginary stones. Jim shook his head. "You've put your best effort into this project, Taylor. We just don't have the money to keep it going while we open casting back up to find a new actress."

Taylor pushed her shoulders back and felt a sense of rightness settle over her. "We don't need to find a new actress. You already have one who knows all the lines and all the marks. Right here."

She saw Trey and Mallory share a smile out of the corner of her eye and the crew's eyes widened in surprise.

"Hell yeah!" Grant shouted as he shot her a sly smile that showed he was mostly kidding. Taylor was sure he was envisioning the pictures of them together at all the promotional events, too.

"Well then, don't just stand there," Jim bellowed. "We're starting the reshoot in one hour. Get the cameras ready. Set up the diner. And you," Jim pointed to a set of orange pigtails hiding behind a rack of clothes. "Find thirty extras and get them to wardrobe. You have twenty minutes."

Cyndi Lu leaned around the clothes and pointed at herself. "Me?"

"You've been hanging around enough, I might as well put you to work."

"Yes, sir!" Cyndi Lu shot an excited smile to Taylor and ran from the room so quickly that she missed Taylor returning a reassuring smile.

"You ready for this?" Trey asked quietly as the room sprang into action.

"More than anything. I have this feeling in my heart that this is the right thing to do. I almost can't wait to get started. I kept showing Melanie how I wanted scenes done and the passion flared up. It couldn't have happened without your support. Thank you for believing in me." Taylor rose on her toes and placed a gentle kiss on his lips.

"I love you, Taylor. And I'm so proud of you," Trey told her as he cupped her face between his hands.

"What the hell are you doing?" Jim yelled. "Get your ass into make-up! Just because you're the producer and a la-di-da Academy Award-winning actress doesn't mean you get to goof off. Now move it!"

"Yes, sir!" Taylor said with a smile that lit the whole room. She tossed a wink to Trey before heading to the make-up trailer with more excitement that she ever felt before.

Trey looked to Mallory. She'd already started to follow Taylor when he called out to her. "I know the threat is over, but could you stay the day and help me with something?"

"Sure. I was going to talk to her while she was in make-up about not needing me any longer. I can send one of my other guys for crowd control if you'd like. I was also going to let her know her parents flew back to L.A. last night."

"That's a relief. And I would talk to her about bringing on some of your guys. See if Taylor will let the production company hire your company for security. But first, I need to run some errands and I need you to text me when things are wrapping up here."

"Sure," Mallory said before sauntering off with Grant trailing behind her. Trey grimaced as Grant gave Mallory a pat on the bottom. Mallory spun so quickly that Trey almost missed the glint of a blade she held pressed against Grant's privates. She said something so quietly that nobody but Grant could hear. Based on his reaction, it didn't take much imagination to know what was said.

Trey shielded the sun from his eyes with his hand as he watched the plane land on the private airstrip near the

Vultures' stadium. The plane rolled to a stop and a few minutes later the door was open and steps rolled down. He kept his eye on the door and smiled when the first orthopedic shoe appeared. His help had arrived.

"Yoo-hoo!" Miss Lily waved as Miss Daisy and Miss Violet peeked around her.

"Get a move on, Lily Rae. I think a mosquito the size of a Buick just landed on me," Miss Daisy complained as she sprayed some bug spray around her.

"I brought food!" Miss Violet called.

"I brought the town!" Miss Lily shot back.

"I brought the bug spray!" Miss Daisy sprayed again as they headed down the stairs of the plane. Behind them, Reagan and Riley were practically dancing in place waiting to get off the plane.

"Mr. Everett! We have our pretty dresses with us!" they called as they ran down the steps.

"And I have flowers—tons and tons of flowers from my grandma's garden." Katelyn called as she, Gemma, Cy, and Marshall came down the stairs slowly carrying boxes filled with flowers.

"And I have my harp," Ryan Hall said proudly as he followed them down the stairs.

"Ryan?" Trey hurried over to his fellow Keeneston High School football player. "Aren't you in summer training?" Ryan played for Tennessee in the NFL.

"We picked him up along the way. Miss Lily insisted there be a harp for the proposal," Mo said smoothly as he and Dani descended.

"Harp? You don't play the harp," Trey said slightly confused.

Ryan shrugged. "I picked it up two years ago during off-season. Coach wanted me to find something to help with my catching. Turns out playing the harp for a wide receiver is like taking ballet for running backs and quarterbacks. I got you hooked up. Learned Handel's *Harp Concerto.*" Ryan and Trey fist-bumped before Ryan moved to help unload his harp.

"And we have everything we need to arrange the perfect ambience," Kenna said excitedly as she and Will carried a huge box down the steep steps.

"And I have the flower baskets that grandma made," Sienna called down, showing off three baskets with different-colored ribbons laced in and out of the woven wood.

"Wow." Trey couldn't think of anything else to say. He stood staring at the people he'd grown up with, all there to help him. "When I asked for help, I thought you'd just give me some advice."

"The Rose sisters are more *doers*. Besides, today is their day on the engagement bet." Ahmed shrugged as he carried a sleepy Abby down the stairs in front of Bridget.

"That's right. And we brought the zip ties," Bridget held up bags of ties and grinned. "I guess I'll be just as good at tying up flowers as bad guys."

"You'll do wonderfully, my dear, just like you do on everything," Ahmed slid his arm around his wife as Abby snuggled against his chest.

"So, Miss Lily said you had a plan," Will said as they all gathered around.

"Yup." Trey couldn't stop grinning. He had the perfect proposal planned. "We're spending the day at the beach."

"Cut! That was freaking fantastic!" Jim yelled as the crew applauded and Cyndi Lu bounced excitedly by his side.

Grant picked Taylor up and swung her around. "Damn, I hate what happened. I'm so glad you're back. Our chemistry is insane. But then again, who could resist me?"

"I know! I just close my eyes and think it's Trey and I can tolerate working with you," Taylor teased. They had gotten more shots done that day than they had in the previous week. They were still behind, but a few more days like this and they would be caught up.

"I'm glad I can be of some use to the movie." Taylor turned and saw Trey leaning against the door with his arms crossed over his chest.

"Oh my gosh, Trey!" Taylor leaped into his arms and hugged him. "I did it. It was so much fun. I can't believe I waited this long. This story and knowing I have some power over it is perfect," Taylor gushed.

"I can't wait to hear about it. Go change and we'll go for a walk on the beach. You can tell me all about it then."

"Oh, that sounds fantastic. I'll be just a minute." Taylor gave him a quick kiss and then hurried to the make-up trailer to change.

Taylor kicked off her sandals and squished her toes in the sand. The Hung Island treasure hadn't been found last night and today the beach seemed empty. Which was just perfect for her and Trey as they linked fingers and walked along the beach enjoying the sunset.

"I can hardly contain myself," Taylor squealed. "It was so awesome. The rush from knowing I did a good job and that the film is going to be a success . . . I'm just so proud of myself. Is that silly?"

"Not at all. Strength comes in many forms, not just physical. You are a strong woman, Taylor. Strong enough to stand by me for all these years when I've gotten banged and bruised on the field. Strong enough to stand up to your parents and start living your own life. Strong enough to admit when you needed help from Jim on the directing and producing. Strong enough to start your own business. And strong enough to overcome your fear and step back in front of the camera. You are the strongest woman I know and I'm so proud of you."

Taylor felt her knees go weak. Trey loved her. He told her that all the time, but he was also a gentleman of few words. He'd never been so passionate before and it sent her heart soaring. They rounded a curve in the beach and Trey pulled her to him. She looked up in his eyes and saw resolve.

"But there is one thing I have not done because I didn't feel worthy of someone as special as you. I should have learned to trust in myself as you do in yourself. You inspire me every day."

Taylor felt as if she were living in a dream. The waves washed against the sandy shore as Trey's lips met hers and music played. Could she be anymore in love? When he pulled away from their kiss, she sighed in disappointment. She wanted so much more than just a kiss.

"Come on. We're almost home," Trey whispered against her ear as if he understood what she was thinking.

Taylor opened her eyes and noticed that there actually was music playing. It was soft and lyrical as the notes danced through the air. She was about to ask if Trey heard it when they rounded the corner. Taylor blinked in shock, surprise, and confusion at the scene on the beach. Reagan and Riley Davies, along with their cousin Sydney Davies and Sienna Ashton stood tossing rose petals in the air. An arched trellis filled with flowers framed the brilliant sunset. Taylor darted her eyes around the beach and saw Ryan

Hall, Trey's friend from high school, playing a harp between two sand dunes. And, wait, were those three white heads popping out behind one of the dunes?

"Taylor," Trey said quietly as he guided her up the rose-petaled aisle the girls had created. She stopped under the trellis in disbelief. The smell of flowers mixed in the air with the soft music, and she felt her heart beat wildly against her chest when Trey went down on one knee.

"You deserve so much more than a country boy like me, but I promise no one will love you as much as I do. I fell in love with you by the pond in Keeneston the night we first met, and I've spent these past years falling more and more in love with you. Not only do you make me a better man, we make each other stronger. We're a team, a family, and I would love nothing more than to be your husband. Taylor Jefferies, will you marry me?"

Taylor tried to say yes, but happy tears fell as she could only nod her answer. "Yes," she gasped finally. Trey slipped a ring she didn't even see him holding onto her finger before he sprang up, wrapping her in a tight hug. He then gave her a kiss that showed her all the love he felt.

The sound of applause had them breaking apart.

"Did she say yes, Daddy?" little Abby asked.

"Yes, my dear, she did," Ahmed said with Abby wrapped around his neck and Bridget held against his side.

The Roses dabbed the tears in their eyes and Ryan broke out the Keeneston High School fight song on the harp as Taylor and Trey became surrounded.

"Uncle Cy!" Taylor wrapped her arms around the person who had practically raised her. "What are you all doing here?"

"Someone had to come give his blessing. And you know the rest wanted to lord it over the town that they witnessed your engagement."

"Your blessing?" Taylor looked between a smiling Trey and Cy.

"That's right. Trey came to Keeneston to ask my permission to marry you. He knew I might shoot him if he didn't. And being the gentleman that he is, he got permission from the whole town. You have a lot of people looking out for you, Taylor."

Taylor felt the tears fall again as everyone nodded their agreement. "And," Gemma started before stepping forward with Katelyn, Kenna, Bridget, and Dani. "We ladies were also hoping you'd let us aunts take you dress shopping."

"And if it's alright with you, we would like to throw you a shower," Miss Violet said before pulling her down in a tight hug.

"And we've been practicing being flower girls along with Layne and Piper!" the girls cried excitedly as they tossed petals in the air.

"I don't know what to say. Yes, to all of you," Taylor laughed before she spotted her new friend standing a little way behind them. "Oh, Mallory! You have to come, too."

Mallory stepped forward and the Keeneston group moved so that she could give Taylor a hug. "I'd love to, especially if these are the guys that come out of Keeneston. When do you think you'll get married?"

Taylor shrugged as she looked up at Trey. It didn't matter. She had everything she wanted right now.

"That settles it," Miss Lily stated as she drew all the attention to her. "Call Father James. We need to set a date or it'll never happen. Violet Fae, start coming up with a menu. Ladies, pick a date for dress shopping. Ryan!"

The harp music stopped and all six-foot-four inches came running over. "Yes, ma'am?"

"Pick a date that doesn't interfere with football season. Let's get this show on the road. We have a wedding to plan!" Miss Lily stopped and looked at the happy couple. Trey's arms were wrapped around Taylor's lower waist and they were staring lost into each other's eyes. "And it better be soon by the looks of it."

Trey felt nothing but pure happiness. He let the town start planning their wedding, knowing they would do right by them. Leaning down, he brought his lips to his future wife's ear. "No one realizes it, but I just found Hung Island's treasure. You."

Taylor tossed her head back and laughed. "And I found it in you. I love you, Trey."

Mallory stood quietly by the sand dune watching the happy celebration and waiting. She wondered if he'd remembered her. When he suddenly appeared by her side, she had her answer.

"Miss Westin, such a pleasure to see you again. And under much better circumstances."

"And you, Ahmed. It's always nice to see each other when someone isn't shooting at you. You have a beautiful family."

"Thank you. I am very blessed. You?"

"No. Still cursed in the love department. Kicking ass in the security department, though. That time we worked together did wonders for my business."

"People just needed to see you as more than a pretty face."

"Flatterer. It had nothing to do with my face and everything to do with my father. Thank you for all you did. You didn't have to."

With a small bow of his head, he walked back into the

crowd. His wife smiled as he picked his daughter up and pretended to throw her in the ocean. Her giggles reached Mallory's ears and tore at her heart. She'd never have that at the rate her relationships were going.

Her phone beeped and she pulled it out of her pocket to read the text message from her best friend, Elle. *Bree's been hurt. She's in the hospital. I'm heading there now. Hurry.* Mallory felt the blood drain from her body. The Simpson family was more of a family to her than her own. She wouldn't forgive herself if something happened to one of them. She'd just been working with Bree. Without a second thought, she walked sure and steady into the happy crowd. She found her target and stopped next to him.

Lowering her voice so the others couldn't hear, she got his attention. "Excuse me, Your Highness. My name is Mallory Westin. I once worked with Ahmed to save your life and I need to borrow your plane."

The End

About the Author

Kathleen Brooks is a New York Times, Wall Street Journal, and USA Today bestselling author. Kathleen's stories are romantic suspense featuring strong female heroines, humor, and happily-ever-afters. Her Bluegrass Series and follow-up Bluegrass Brothers Series feature small town charm with quirky characters that have captured the hearts of readers around the world.

Kathleen is an animal lover who supports rescue organizations and other non-profit organizations such as Friends and Vets Helping Pets whose goals are to protect and save our four-legged family members.

Email Notice of New Releases:
www.kathleen-brooks.com/new-release-notifications/

Kathleen's Website:
www.kathleen-brooks.com

Facebook Page:
www.facebook.com/KathleenBrooksAuthor

Twitter:
www.twitter.com/BluegrassBrooks

Goodreads:
www.goodreads.com/author/show/5101707.Kathleen_Brooks

GOOD NEWS FOR FANS OF KEEENESTON!

In addition to *All Hung Up,* more Bluegrass Singles will be released in the coming year. Jake & Marcy's story, *Bluegrass Dawn*, has a target release date in late November. Much more info will be made available soon on my website.

Sign up at this link to receive notification for all new releases by Kathleen Brooks: www.kathleen-brooks.com/new-release-notifications/

If you are new to the writings of Kathleen Brooks, then you will definitely want to try her Bluegrass Series books set in the wonderful fictitious town of Keeneston, KY. Here is a list of links to the Bluegrass and Bluegrass Brothers books in order:

Bluegrass Series

Bluegrass State of Mind

Risky Shot

Dead Heat

Bluegrass Brothers Series

Bluegrass Undercover

Rising Storm

Secret Santa, A Bluegrass Novella

Acquiring Trouble

Relentless Pursuit

Secrets Collide

Final Vow

Bluegrass Singles

All Hung Up

Bluegrass Dawn – coming November of 2014

Women of Power Series

Chosen for Power

Built for Power

Fashioned for Power – coming early 2015

Made in the USA
Monee, IL
26 January 2020